T0171726

Adventures around the World

Tibor Vajda

iUniverse, Inc.
Bloomington

Adventures around the World

iUniverse books may be ordered through booksellers or by contacting:

iUniverse
1663 Liberty Drive
Bloomington, IN 47403
www.iuniverse.com
1-800-Authors (1-800-288-4677)

ISBN: 978-1-4620-7150-0 (sc)
ISBN: 978-1-4620-7151-7 (e)

Printed in the United States of America

iUniverse rev. date: 12/08/2011

To my wife for being here with me.
Grateful thanks to Penelope Grace for her assisting in editing.

Contents

Target Buenos Aires.

Chapter I.

SWISSWELL, AN INTENATIONAL PHARMACEUTICAL firm, released a new anti-malaria drug on the market. One vaccine was supposed to provide immunity against malaria for a life-time. The drug 'Antimal' was introduced at a medical conference, 'Drugs for infectious diseases', for foreign doctors in Lausanne, Switzerland.

Of the 300 participants, a Hungarian doctor, Andrew Mady, outshone the others with his knowledgeable comments and practical suggestions for the marketing of the drug worldwide. Before the end of the conference the Vice-President of the Company, Mr Lafarge, who was responsible for security, invited Mady to a private dinner party.

At the party Mady, who was seated next to Mr Lafarge, sketched on paper serviettes a provisional map showing the order in which the various continents - Africa, Asia, South America - should be 'attacked' by giving demonstrations and by subsidizing doctors working in small to medium hospitals.

Lafarge, who had a say in recruiting new associates, offered Mady an interview the next morning, which he accepted. At the meeting Lafarge offered him 'associate' status in Swisswell with considerable annual wages. Mady accepted the offer and they agreed that Mady's first assignment would be to produce a discussion paper on the best way to market 'Antimal' worldwide. Lafarge also offered to pay Mady's expenses so he could stay two more days in Lausanne to study and discuss relevant problems with employees of Swisswell and also collect confidential information provided by the company to help his future work.

Mady could not accept the two days offer, pointing out that in Hungary, under the Communist government, he was not supposed to make changes to the previously approved travel schedule and warned Lafarge that his employment by Swisswell would have to be kept secret.

Lafarge wanted to know if Mady would be able to travel overseas to promote 'Antimal' himself. Mady told him that though his chances for overseas travel would be limited, he hoped to make some trips, using his connections in the medical profession and in the pharmaceutical trade. As an example, he mentioned that just before coming to Lausanne he had received an invitation to a medical conference in Buenos Aires from the 24 to 30 July 1971, and perhaps because he was offered the Vice-Chairmanship of the conference, his trip to Buenos Aires had been approved by the Minister for Health.

They agreed that Lafarge would arrange a visit to Budapest to discuss with Hungarian companies possible cooperation in their new products in the pipeline and while in Budapest they would be able to discuss the next steps for Mady to work for Swisswell.

The forty year old Mady has never travelled outside Europe and while his German and English were alright, he spoke no Spanish. Considering his future meetings with South American colleagues, he started taking lessons with a Spanish tutor in Budapest and bought a good Spanish language book to take with him and study during his trip to Buenos Aires.

Mady's trip from Budapest via London, Tahiti, Easter Island and Santiago to Buenos Aires took more than 24 hours, passing through many time-zones. He had to change planes in London, from Swiss Air to Aerolineas of Argentina, but the further stops were only for refuelling. That gave Mady an opportunity to stretch his legs and look around the airport buildings. The Argentine Conference paid Mady's airfare, but although he had a business class ticket he felt cramped with his long legs during the flight.

Chapter II.

AFTER COLLECTING HIS SINGLE suitcase at the Buenos Aires airport he was surprised to see a middle-aged couple holding a small sign with his name. After the usual greetings they were all in for a surprise. The couple were Dr Bakos and his wife, Hungarian migrants, who had left Hungary in 1944 with the German army and emigrated to Argentina with the help of the Catholic Rescue Mission in Vienna.

Doctor Bakos' first question to Mady was strange; "Did you play tennis on the Duna tennis courts in Budapest before the war?" Mady replied that he hadn't. Then the misunderstanding was cleared up. Bakos used to play tennis at the Duna courts with one "Mady", a young member of the aristocratic Mady family and when he heard that Dr Mady was coming to Buenos Aires, he offered to meet 'his former tennis partner' at the airport.

Andrew Mady explained that he was indeed a member of the well-known Mady family but he belonged to the family's impoverished branch. After the confusion and Bakos' embarrassment was cleared up, they took Mady to his hotel, the Claridge, were he had a room booked by the Conference.

Claridge was one of the older hotels of Buenos Aires but it had been restored. The two Greek columns supporting the entrance were painted stark white. The floor of the spacious lobby was marble. The reception desk and all furniture in the lobby were dark wood. The whole building was air-conditioned and they had good service for the guests, as the Bakos couple assured Mady.

It was about 7 p.m. by the time Mady settled down in his room. He felt tired and sleepy after the long flight, so he undressed and lay down.

To his surprise sleep didn't come easily, despite keeping his eyes tightly closed. Hoping that it would help him sleep, he got out of bed and took a hot bath in the en suite bathroom and went back to bed. Frustrated, he felt even more awake than before the bath.

I must get a good night's sleep before tomorrow morning, so I function properly and put to use my less than perfect Spanish. I have to exhaust myself, so I can fall asleep, he decided. He rejected the idea of taking a sleeping pill, to avoid getting sleepy in the morning when he expected to meet his colleagues. With a sudden idea, he got dressed and left the hotel, thinking that a brisk walk in the cool evening air would do the trick and help him get to sleep.

It was only 9.30 p.m. when he stepped on the street. Instinctively he turned to the left remembering that they had come from that direction when they'd turned into the hotel's street. He found himself on a wide boulevard, street-lights blazing and shop-windows brightly lit.

Where to now? A neon sign with an arrow pointed to the street opposite the hotel. The sign said "Ca' Doro". *It has to be a night club,* Mady thought, and without much ado he headed in that direction.

Did Mady wish to go into a night club? Probably not. He didn't even take his wallet when he left the hotel. He just realized that when he felt his pockets. He saw the bright lights of Ca'Doro and a display window with pictures of almost naked girls. He also saw the sign; "Club opens at 10 p.m."

It was only 9.45 p.m. and Mady already felt exhausted. The walk in the fresh air after the tiresome flight had finally caught up with him. He turned, went back to the hotel and fell asleep minutes after lying down on his bed.

Chapter III.

- -

THE NEXT DAY, MONDAY, Mady got up at 9 a.m. He had a shower and went to have breakfast in the hotel cafeteria. After having his coffee and hard boiled eggs, he remembered that he didn't have any Argentine currency and that the Bakos couple had promised to come and fetch him at 11 a.m. He went to the reception where the currency exchange prices were displayed and changed 200 US Dollars into pesos. It was almost half of the 500 Dollars he had for his whole stay on the trip. He did count on getting back his expenses for the trip from Swisswell after returning home but was not sure how he would manage on his 500 Dollars. He sighed when this passed through his mind.

The Bakoses arrived at 11 a.m. and suggested showing Mady a little bit around the city. "By the way," said Dr Bakos, "if you need pesos, don't change your money at the hotel. I could change it for you for 50% more than they would." "Okay," said Mady, who was ashamed to admit that he had just made that mistake.

Bakos left his car in the hotel garage and they went on foot toward the city centre. First they turned into the Florida, one of the oldest avenues of Buenos Aires. The street scene reminded Mady of Vaczi Street in Budapest. All along it there were fashion shops for men or women, displaying hats, shoes and underwear in the latest styles. Mady assumed that everything in the shops would be very expensive but Bakos told him that in fact these elegant shops were not more expensive that any others. Bakos pointed out a pair of shoes with the price marked at 24 dollars. That was about half the price Mady would have expected.

Then there was a string of restaurants, old-fashioned or modern, one after the other. Bakos pointed out the sign TORTINERI and offered

7

Mady a real good espresso coffee in there. Mady refused because he had already had a coffee at the hotel.

Then, just as if fate had arranged it for Mady, a local pair dressed in Argentine folk costumes demonstrated the 'tango' to the accompaniment of an accordion.

Walking on down the Florida they arrived at the Plaza 5. Mayo. There was plenty to admire there, as Bakos proudly pointed out the historical buildings around the large circular plaza.

On the corner of Florida was the 'Galleria Pacifico', a permanent exhibition of local artists. Opposite was the magnificent 'Casa Rosada', the Argentine Parliament. "The locals call it the most useless building in Argentina, because nothing happens there," said Bakos, laughing. The huge, all-pink marble building reminded Mady of the USA Capitol Building with its cupola.

On one side of the Plaza there was an old Spanish style, white-washed building with a tower, and with artistic, black iron grilles on every window and door. "That must be a church," said Mady to Bakos, only to be corrected; "It is the Trade Union Centre".

After looking around and getting told about all the famous landmarks, Mady realized that it was already 12.30 p.m. "We have to be at the opening of the Congress at 1 p.m.," Mady reminded Bakos, who just smiled. "We still have plenty of time to get to the Hypodrom," which prompted Mady to ask, "Actually, why is the opening lunch of the Medical Congress in a Hypodrom?"

"Well, there is a large, elegant Festival Hall at the Hypodrom, not far from the races, where international conferences are usually held. Besides, after the lunch there will be a parade and exhibition of horsemanship by a unit of the Mounted Police." *I don't think this could happen in any other country,* passed through Mady's mind.

The Hypodrom's Festival Hall was no different from any other banquet hall Mady had ever seen or imagined. There were long tables with small flags, signalling all the countries the participating delegates came from. Mady soon found out that consular officials of those countries had also attended the lunch.

Bakos, who was not a delegate, just an official of the organizing committee, pushed Mady forward saying, "Look for your flag. That's where you will sit". Within minutes, Mady had two big surprises: one, that the Hungarian flag marking his place had the 'St. Istvan shield and crown' on it, which had been removed years before in Communist

Hungary; two, that an elegant lady and a man in old Hungarian uniform of the 'Order of Vitez' - established by Governor Horthy and also dissolved by Communist Hungary - were sitting on the chairs next to the Hungarian flag. The man, in his 60s, stood and presented Mady with a business card.

"Doctor Semsey Andor, Hungarian Consul and Comtesse Semsey nee Comtesse Karolyi." The man offered his hand and then the Comtesse stood and offered her hand to Mady, holding it so high, close to Mady's mouth, that it would have been obvious to anybody that she expected him to kiss her hand rather than shake it.

Mady, who was of a new generation and never saw men kissing women's hands, first tried to shake the hand but then the Comtesse lifted her hand almost to Mady's mouth which gave even him no chance to do other than to kiss it. Mady couldn't believe his eyes.

Could Hungarian aristocrats, pushed out of all state positions at home, be still representing Hungary overseas? he asked himself.

Later Bakos explained that the Argentine government refused to accept the new Ambassador and Consul nominations of the Communist Hungarian government and so Hungary was still represented in Argentina by people delegated by Admiral Horthy before the war. "It was an impasse," said Bakos.

It took some time for Mady to understand why there were small, square ceramic stands of two levels in front of everyone's place at the table. *They couldn't possibly use them to heat up food on the dinner table?* he wondered. Then he found out that they were used for exactly that purpose. The waiters went around and placed choice meet cuts on the burning hot ceramic stands.

When Mady asked Semsey where this strange 'facility' came from he was told that Argentine people were different from all other people when it came to meat consumption. "They not only eat the steaks but all the innards too and it was considered normal for an Argentine man to eat two kilograms of meat a day."

After the meal and the consumption of the strong black coffee, the President of the Congress, Doctor Pedro Bocchi, gave a short speech about the significance of the Congress on Infectious Diseases and called out the names of all the countries participating. For Mady, the list seemed never ending. Almost 200 countries were represented. Mady eagerly waited for the name of the Argentine delegate; "Glauco Longo", the man he was supposed to find and contact.

Chapter IV.

AFTER THE LAUSANNE INTERNATIONAL Conference, Mr Lafarge reported to Leon Adler, the Executive Director of Swisswell, that he trusted Dr Mady of Hungary to investigate Glauco Longo, Argentine research worker. According to a Swissell's confidant in the World Health Organisation, Longo submitted a patent and trade mark application almost identical to Swisswell's 'Antimal' application.

The Patent Organization couldn't reject Longo's application for 'Malantin' but delayed its acceptance for three months on the basis of asking Longo for better details. "We have three months to buy or destroy this Longo and his 'Malantin'," Lafarge told to Adler.

"Do you think somebody affiliated with our research laboratory, a member of the research team, or even a cleaner could have passed on some data that helped Longo to be competitive with us?" asked Adler.

Lafarge explained that there were three associates working on the 'Antimal' project: two Swiss males and one woman who became a Swiss citizen after she divorced her husband in Munich, where she used to work with Bayer laboratories. In general the security of the building and particularly the security of the research laboratory was considered excellent by experts of the Swiss Counter Intelligence.

"What do you suggest we should do, Mr Lafarge?" asked Adler.

"As a matter of urgency I will organize a general security raid with the help of friendly State Security people and employ a Swiss private detective to check all details of the lives of the three research associates," suggested Lafarge. Adler agreed and asked Lafarge to keep him informed of the ongoing investigation and reminded him that they had a very short time to do something 'drastic', because Swisswell could not afford to lose the millions of dollars already invested in the project and the possible loss of the expected worldwide income from the 'Antimal' marketing.

Lafarge received the first report from the private detective. The two Swiss men seemed to be beyond suspicion but Gisele Huper, the third associate, was not so clear.

Huper was German by birth. She had married the Argentine chemist, Glauco Longo, in Munich, who also worked at the Bayer Company. About ten years ago, after a stormy divorce which figured prominently in the newspapers, the husband left Germany and took the couple's small son with him, while Gisele Huper was actually fired from Bayer. She then moved to Switzerland where, after the obligatory waiting time, she became Swiss citizen.

According to an unconfirmed article in one of the smaller German papers, Huper was suspected of using drugs at the time, obtained at the Company where she worked.

There was something especially suspicious, according to the detective. Huper had taken her annual leave of four weeks a fortnight ago. She said to co-workers that she intended to visit South America, more precisely Venezuela, where she hoped to see the magnificent Iguacu Falls. She had been planning to see the Falls for a long time, after seeing pictures of them in the movies.

"Can you check if Huper crossed from Venezuela to Argentina?" Lafarge asked the detective. He had a feeling that following Huper would lead to the leak of the vital information about Antimal. "We sure can," answered the detective and promised an early report on Huper's trip.

In less than a week the detective reported to Lafarge that Huper received a visa to Argenina at the Caracas Embassy the day after she arrived there. "We were lucky," said the detective, "because Huper left a forwarding Buenos Aires address at the Embassy. It is," said the detective looking into his papers, "Villa Ballesteros, Avenida General Vitadello No.9. An outer suburb of Buenos Aires."

"Can you send a Spanish speaking agent to Buenos Aires?"

"Sure, but what is our man supposed to do there?"

"He should keep Huper under surveillance and report back what is she doing there and mainly who is she meeting with. Locals, or foreigners? There is an International Medical Congress there, you know. Lafarge deliberately didn't mention the name of Glauco Longo, the man they were most interested in. He wanted the detective to come up with his name as Huper's contact. "Keep in mind that this mission is urgent!" He told the detective forcefully.

Chapter V.

AFTER DOCTOR BOCCHI'S SPEECH some of the delegates stood and started to leave. *How come?* wondered Mady. There was supposed to be a spectacular presentation of horsemanship by the Police. That was the explanation for using the Hypodrom.

"Oh, you didn't know? There is a revolution in Cordoba and the Police Riding Unit got stuck there. There will be no riding exhibition," said Semsey and turned away before Mady could ask him how he would get to the Palacio Congreso of the Congress. *Where is Bakos? He has to be here somewhere,* thought Mady and started to look for his 'guide'.

Bakos took Mady back to the hotel and in the meantime showed him how to get to the Congress from the Claridge by walking just about five minutes.

Mady had a short nap then took a shower. Walking to the Congress building took him only five minutes indeed. To his surprise, the Palacio Congreso building looked like a large hangar from the outside. However the inside was very different. Mady's first reaction was that the semicircular interior with lines of seats on the ground and boxes with three seats on the balconies supported by elegant black marble columns, looked like an elegant theatre rather than a Congress venue.

Mady halfexpected to find that seats were allocated for every delegate and started looking for name cards but soon realized that everybody could take any of the unoccupied seats. He chose a 'dress circle' box, opposite the stage, and sat on one of the three empty seats. It proved to be a lucky choice.

The first man to join him in the box was Lindsay Cabral from Brazil and the second was none other than Glauco Longo, the man he was supposed to contact. After short introductions, they started to speak about generalities, like how beautiful the Palacio Congreso was, as Longo referred to the venue, and expressed their admiration for the organizing committee who managed to bring together the 200 or so professionals involved in fighting infectious diseases from practically every part of the world.

The presidency of the Congress took their places at the table on the stage and the meeting was opened at 10.30 a.m., a mere half an hour later than officially planned. Mady made a light-hearted remark about the delay but Longo mentioned that this half an hour delay was nothing compared to the usual delays one experienced in Buenos Aires. "These people don't seem to have any idea of punctuality," he said, then added, "I must be a rare exception." Those, who expected a long speech from the President, Pedro Bocchi, were disappointed. Bocchi greeted the delegates, and announced they had 200 professionals attending from all over the world.

Bocchi then thanked the Pharmaceutical companies, Pfizer, Merck and Hoechts for underwriting the considerable expenses involved in the organization. He explained that there would be stalls set up in the foyer where during the breaks the delegates could obtain free samples and also get expert explanations from the companies' representatives about their latest products.

Bocchi finally announced that delegates on the programme would have 15 minutes each for their presentations - with slides – to introduce their work. Delegates from Africa – the Republic of Congo - and from Asia – Thailand – would say a few words of interest to everybody.

The African delegate took the rostrum and explained that in his and in other African countries the fight against malaria and billharzia was very important. He quoted statistical figures about the increase of those diseases despite government organized campaigns to eradicate them. "We need cheaper, easily obtainable drugs to turn this alarming trend around," he concluded.

The delegate from Thailand presented his country's fight against malaria and dengue fever. He joined the African delegate's request for cheaper, easily obtainable drugs against all parasitic infectious diseases.

"Well, I hope this Congress will produce some new methods, some new medicine to help to eradicate those infectious diseases. That's our programme," said Longo then turned to Mady; "You don't have these problems in the middle of Europe, I imagine."

"We are not completely free of these problems in Hungary, though in our continental country these parasites spreading diseases are not prevalent in alarming numbers. We have malaria infestations in the swampy areas south of Lake Balaton and I'm here to pick up methods and drugs we can employ to defeat these diseases."

"What about your pharmaceutical companies and medical research teams? Aren't they conducting research in these fields?" asked Cabral.

"It seems that they rather hope to import suitable drugs to treat those, while they are concentrating on research for painkillers," Mady told him.

Chapter VI.

AFTER A SMALL NUMBER of presentations the Congress adjourned to the following morning. Cabral asked Mady and Longo what were their plans for the rest of the evening. They told him they had no further plans, after all it was already 9.15 p.m.

"Don't you think we should show our Hungarian colleague something special, like the Boca?" Cabral asked Longo. "Who knows if he'll have another chance to see Buenos Aires."

Cabral, who seemed to take a shine to Mady as soon as they met, insisted that they should go as his guests to the Boca, which was, according to him, the entertainment centre of the capital.

As soon as Mady heard the name Boca, he remembered that his Spanish teacher in Budapest warned him not to go to the Boca because that is the worst part of Buenos Aires, infamous for the criminals who live there and the daily murders which happen there, according to her information.

Cabral laughed off Mady's idea of the Boca, asking him; "Would I invite you there, if there was any substance to that story?"

The visit to the Boca was an experience for Mady. They took a taxi there just before 10 p.m. Even in the poor street lighting he could see strange looking timber houses, painted in various bright colours, yellow, red, sky blue. The streets were deserted. The cab stopped at the bright neon signs of the Spada Vecchia restaurant. It was a large building. Inside, every table seemed to be occupied. Samba music blared and the waiters moved skilfully between tables, singing loudly the melodies the band played.

Elegant pairs vigorously danced the samba on the large dance floor. Cabral ordered fish for dinner and he suggested they all try the spicy dish. He was right, Mady did like it. The Chilean white wine, ordered by Cabral, was to Mady's taste too. Despite Cabral's encouragement, Mady resisted the inviting glances of some pretty ladies to dance.

They left after midnight which gave Cabral enough time to tell Mady about his work - he was a pathologist working for the Police - and about his family. He had a German wife and they had a six-month-old baby. They lived in Rio de Janeiro and he promptly invited Mady to visit them in Rio after the Congress. Mady politely refused the invitation knowing that he had other things to do.

Tuesday morning Mady walked alone from the Claridge at Tucuman Avenue to the Congress. Cabral and Longo were already sitting in their seats and cheerfully greeted Mady, asking if he had a good sleep after the late night.

It was already 10.30 a.m. when the first presentation started, half an hour later then it was supposed to start. When Mady mentioned this, Longo told him that he should get used to the lack of punctuality in Argentina. Mady remembered Longo's words in the following days when everything and everybody was late for pre-arranged meetings.

During the presentations, Longo asked Mady what his main interest was. Was it 'prevention', such as chemically treating areas frequented by the parasites, or was it 'treatment' of infected people?

"Your question covers two large areas. Being a medical practitioner I'm mainly involved in the 'treatment', the 'healing' part," answered Mady. "And what is your area?" he asked back.

"I'm working in both areas. To me, the prevention and healing parts are closely related and have to be part of one grand design to eradicate all parasitic infectious diseases. That's what this Congress is supposed to be about."

Mady decided this was the moment to get closer to Longo, and find out about his research.

"It seems to me that you, Doctor Longo, are deeply involved in this field. How come you are not making a presentation? Don't you have enough material yet to show it to the world, or are you protecting your research results from unscrupulous people?"

"Neither," answered Longo. "I have actually achieved my goal and within the next few months I will get both patent and trade mark for my innovation. It will be then available to every country, including Hungary, 'at a price', of course."

Mady decided not to press Longo further at this stage. "Are you saying that the big pharmaceutical companies, like the ones present, have no idea about your results yet?"

"Indeed they haven't. I believe in doing everything the right way and at the right time. I keep mum about my results until I've got the patent, then maybe I will take it to a special auction. Let the big boys fight for the results of my years long, backbreaking work," said Longo. Mady decided not to press Longo further because they were not alone. *Who the hell is this Doctor Lindsay Cabral? Maybe he is working for the enemy?* he thought and decided to look for an occasion when they would be alone.

In the lunch break Longo invited Mady and Cabral to be his guests at a Churrasco restaurant on Avenida 9 de Julio, not far from the Congress. "You can have there choice pieces of grilled steak, marinated with any spice you like, and served with fresh salad. By the way, the Avenida itself is worth a look by somebody visiting this city for the first time. The Avenida 9 de Julio is the longest and widest Avenida in the world!"

The three crossed a park where the Avenida began. Mady noticed that a number of police cars and firemen moved around a Bank's entrance. Many people were hanging around, watching what the police were doing. Mady asked Longo what had happened and he was told, "There must have been a robbery."

"In the middle of the city, in daylight?" asked an incredulous Mady.

"Yes, it is not unusual here," was Longo's answer. He was completely uninterested and moved on, toward the restaurant.

The steaks were huge and well prepared, according to the guest's wishes. Mady never thought he could eat so much meat in one sitting but wanted to keep up with the other two. Besides, the meals tasted very good. Just when he told himself, *I won't eat another thing,* Longo insisted that the other two should be his guests for the evening.

"There is a wonderful restaurant on the Costa Nera Sur, called Costanera. It is at the bay of the Rio Plata River. On a clear day you can see across the bay to Montevideo, on the opposite shore. I will pick you up at 9.30 p.m. and we'll drive there." They all agreed to go. *I never considered one of the dangers of this job that I'd have to eat myself to death,* thought Mady ironically.

After drinking excellent wine, maybe a bit more than he should have, Mady, who couldn't proceed with questioning Longo about his research because of Cabral's presence, asked Longo a question to which he couldn't guess the answer.

"We in Europe," he deliberately didn't say in Hungary, "were brought up on the thesis that Military Dictatorship in any country always means that it is a 'right wing' system. I heard here that General Perron is very popular and he came to power with the help of the Trade Unions. Is that true?"

"It is true," answered Longo and added, "you shouldn't worry about that," and started to make lewd remarks about the beautiful women sitting around them. *Is he married?* wondered Mady but didn't ask Longo about his family life.

Chapter VII.

WEDNESDAY MORNING THE CONGRESS opened almost an hour later than the official timetable projected. As Mady entered the hall, he noticed that delegates were crowding in groups and discussing something excitedly. "What happened?" Mady asked Longo.

"This is another Argentine special", said Longo calmly. "Tupamaros attacked a police station in a suburb, not far from my place. They tied up the policemen and took away their guns. Nobody was hurt. That's all."

"How could they do that? Who are the Tupamaros? Did this happen before?" asked Mady.

"The Tupamaros are supposedly a left-wing revolutionary movement. It started in neighbouring Uruguay last year. As for their 'revolutionary activities', so far they've become famous only for bank robberies and kidnapping people for ransom. Early this year they kidnapped the head of the FIAT organization here in Buenos Aires. How is that for revolutionary activity?"

"Was this raid on the police in a well populated area?"

"It was in a garden suburb. As I said, it was close to my place, in Villa Ballester."

"You are saying Vizha Bazhester. How do you spell the name?" asked Mady. When Longo spelled the name, Mady corrected him, Viya Bayester, that's how I learned the pronounciation of the 'll' in Spanish."

"You are not in Spain, this is Argentina. You have to learn our way of pronounciation," said Longo, closing the subject. Mady and Cabral accepted Longo's invitation to visit his house in the afternoon. Mady didn't mind doing something useful in the noon to five period. He couldn't get used to the situation that the locals religiously took a siesta between 12 and 5 p.m. Shops were closed, doctors and dentists did not work for five hours daily. *So much wasted time!* thought Mady.

Cabral took the others to Longo's house in Villa Ballester. Mady's impression was that Longo's house could stand in any European city as a family cottage, in a garden suburb. It was a three bedroom house standing in a flower-filled garden.

"Make yourselves comfortable while I prepare some snacks and a good coffee for us," Longo told them.

While Longo was busy in the kitchen, Mady and Cabral looked around. There was a piano in the living room and there were pictures on the piano. Among the numerous photos was a family photo of a young Longo, with a five or six year old boy and a young blonde woman. The woman's hair was plaited and she wore a frock and white blouse of the style of German country women, as Mady recognized.

Longo brought in sandwiches and coffee. When he saw that his guests were examining the pictures, he offered some explanation. "That family picture was taken ten years ago in Germany. The woman was my wife Gisele, the boy is Edoardo. We divorced ten years ago and I came home to the country of my birth, Argentina. Edoardo came with me. He is by now a strapping teenager, a cadet in the Naval Academy."

"Does your ex-wife have any contact with you, or with her son?" Mady thought the time was right to find out if Longo had any contact with Gisele, the research worker at Swisswell.

"We have no contact," said Longo, cutting short Mady's line of inquiry. *Was this an angry reaction?* wondered Mady and decided to wait for another opportunity to do any further probing of Longo's contact with Gisele Huper.

Chapter VIII.

THURSDAY MORNING MADY HAD just finished his breakfast in the hotel when it seemed to him that this so far straightforward situation had suddenly turned upside down. As he was leaving the hotel the receptionist called after him.

"Doctor Mady, you have an international telegram!" and handed it to him. Mady couldn't imagine who might have sent it to him.

"There is another thing, a gentleman wants to see you. He is waiting in the lobby. He didn't want to wake you up when he arrived. He said he'd rather wait."

Without looking at the telegram in his hand, Mady turned and went to the lobby. There was a man sitting, reading a newspaper. He looked about 40. His clothing and hat presented a typical European man. Mady noticed him wearing stout ankle boots worn by European tourists in the mountains. When the man saw Mady coming, he put his paper down, stood and greeted Mady like an old acquaintance.

"Hello Dr Mady, Dr Leon Adler sends you his best wishes." *With this he made it clear where he came from, but what did he, or rather what did Leon Adler want?* Mady invited him into his room to secure the privacy of the discussion.

Sitting in Mady's room, the visitor explained the reason for his visit. "It has been established that Gisele Huper pretended that she was going on a holiday but she actually came to Buenos Aires and is staying with her ex-husband at Villa Ballester. Now that it is obvious that Gisele Huper is the one who leaked material to Longo, we have to speed up the investigation and obtain proof that she committed a theft which could cause Swisswell huge losses.

"We have only two months to obtain proof, before Longo's patent application could be accepted. I came to do my work and to help you in case you have difficulties, particularly if it should be necessary to use physical exertion."

What have I got myself into, went trough Mady's mind. *Am I a doctor or a gangster?*

"I'm Karl Schmidt, Swiss private detective, recommended to Dr Adler by the GHP, the Swiss Security Police. My agency has connections to the BAF, the Argentine Security Organizations," said the the man, when he saw Mady's surprised expression. "I can loan you a gun too for your protection," he said, tapping his pocket, and that proposal frightened Mady even more. "Oh no," he rejected the offer.

"By the way," said Mady, "Longo invited me to his Villa Ballester house yesterday and when I asked him he said he had no contact with his ex-wife."

"He would say that, wouldn't he," was Schmidt's reaction.

Schmidt seemed that he wanted to finish the conversation and said, "I am staying in Hotel San Martin in the city. You can call me there, or leave a message. We shouldn't be seen together. I will keep Longo's house under surveillance to catch the wife visiting him and to follow her to establish where she is staying." With this he left.

It was past 11 a.m. when Mady entered the Palacio Congreso. Longo and Cabral in unison asked him where had he been? "We were worried that you were kidnapped by the Tupamaros. It's very fashionable, you know."

"Was that the first thing that came to your mind? I was busy, I had a visitor at the hotel," said Mady and when he said that he suddenly remembered he had an unread telegram in his pocket. "Excuse me," he told them, he took out the telegram, and turned away to read it. That was when the second big surprise of the morning hit him.

"Andrew, The Medical Board and the Disciplinary Department of the Ministerium for Health started an investigation against you. The charge: "You are a paid employee of a Swiss Pharmaceutical Company. If that is proven, you could be deregistered and could not continue working as a medical practitioner. It is serious! Your assistant, Anna, reported you to the authorities. Be very careful. Regards, Laszlo."

Mady felt dizzy. He had to sit down to prevent himself falling. *Is this possible?* The signature 'Laszlo' meant that his friend Laszlo Pinter was worried about him. Anna? Oh, Mady knew who Anna was. She worked with him for three years as his assistant in the surgery and did everything to attract him and become his lover. Maybe she thought she could even become the wife of the bachelor Mady.

It had to be the injured vanity, revenge for her wasted efforts to seduce me. But would she go this far? Trying to destroy the man who, she thought, had neglected her?

Mady must have gone quite white in the face, because Longo and Cabral asked him in unison, "Bad news?" "No, no. Nothing," murmured Mady to the two, then he got up and walked out. He needed fresh air. He felt he was chocking.

Walking up and down in front of the Palacio Congreso, he tried to think reasonably about his situation. *What should I do? What could I do?* There was nobody here he could turn to for advice.

This could only happen in present Hungary. Jealousy, vanity, revenge. Small people attacking an honest man for their own shortcomings. But I am wrong. This could happen in any country, he corrected himself. I graduated in 1957 together with Zoltan Szabo, the present Minister for Health. Szabo was always jealous of me for my better grades. Anna knew about Szabo's hostility toward me and that may have given her the idea to revenge herself for the imaginary hurts, 'neglects,' she suffered because of me. *Hell has no fury like a woman scorned*, Mady remembered someone saying, but he'd never witnessed it himself.

As the fresh air started to cool his head, his thoughts changed tack. *Technically, Szabo is right! I never thought I was compromising my professional status by agreeing to Swisswell's offer. I should have! So what can I do now that they've caught me out? Should I emigrate, leave Hungary for good? Some people managed to start a new life overseas, even colleagues I knew. But I'm not that kind. As the poet said 'one who changes his country, has to change his heart'! I'm not like that, I'm "Magyar" to the hilt. I have to stand up to the attacks and survive them. But how?*

Well, there are no witnesses to prove that I was employed by Swisswell. I didn't sign any papers and didn't receive any money. In fact I didn't do anything they could use as proof that I became a paid Swisswell employee. This is it! I will go back to Hungary and deny all charges. Anna, of course, will have to go and sell her charms to another doctor.

Chapter IX.

ON FRIDAY MORNING THE program had just finished when Mady returned to his seat. Cabral and Longo got up, said, "See you in the evening," and left. Mady remained alone in the box. He looked around. The delegates were leaving the hall, except one woman. She smiled at Mady and came over to him saying in Spanish, "Ola, I'm Dr Roxana Fernandez, let's go and have lunch. Be my guest. I was watching you all week, looking for a chance to speak to you."

"How are you?" answered Mady in English. He was so surprised by the situation that couldn't think of anything else to say to the Spanish-speaking lady. He hadn't spoken a word to any woman during the Congress so far.

"Don't be so surprised," she said, changing to English, lightly touching his arm. "There is a good restaurant nearby, the Tarentino, where we can chat. You'll be interested to hear what I tell you." With this she took Mady's arm and pulled him out of the hall. She kept chatting on their way to the restaurant.

"Do you know that there is another Medical Congress in town? It is organized by 'Medecin sans frontieres' and financed by the government, not by Pharmaceutical Companies, like this one." She pulled a face, when she said 'this one'. Her facial expression demonstrated that she was disgusted when she referred to Mady's Congress. *But why?* Mady had no idea.

"You should come and participate in our meeting, Dr Mady. I can get an invitation for you from Professor Thiele, our Chairman, in the afternoon. We can meet in the evening, have a good time and I can give you your invitation for tomorrow. What do you say?"

She kept on chatting during the meal, praising the high intellectual level of the presentations at the 'other congress', touching Mady's arm from time to time and flashing her dark eyes invitingly.

She is very sexy, admitted Mady to himself, looking at the elegant young woman dressed in a black skirt with a bolero and a red silk blouse. Her dark hair was fashionably done.

Why shouldn't I go with her? But where? My expenses are paid by this Congress. Is it fair professionally to attend another seemingly competing Congress?

Roxana saw that Mady was uncertain and made another push. She took out a book from her handbag and gave it to Mady. It was titled: "Allergies, the real reason?" The author's name: Professor Thiele. Inside, it has been signed: "To the eminent Dr Andrew Mady," by the professor himself. "You see I've already spoken with him about you and he is looking forward to meeting you.

"To hear Thiele, alone, makes it worth your while to come with me," she said with an enticing look and grabbing Mady's arm. In the meantime they drank up the bottle of red wine ordered by Roxana, who gave her credit card to the waiter, quieting Mady who made a gesture he wanted to pay.

"You are staying at the Claridge, aren't you?" asked Roxana when they'd finished eating and seemed to have run out of conservation topics. I will pick you up at 9 p.m. in the lobby of the Claridge, then we will see where to go to have a good time." Mady agreed and gallantly kissed Roxana's hand which she seemed to appreciate.

After a short nap in his hotel room Mady went to the Palacio Congreso and looked for Dr Diana Pok, one of the organisers. She and her father, also a doctor, were very active keeping the presentations in order. Mady had spoken to them only once, when he reported at the reception desk at the beginning.

Diana Pok was a young woman and she looked surprised when Mady told her about his problem, "I've been invited to attend another Medical Congress. I'm not sure if it is alright to go to another meeting when this Congress was kind enough to invite me and pay my expenses?"

"Who invited you?" asked Diana. "It was Dr Roxana Fernandez," said Mady. "Oh, that woman?" said Diana Pok with a deprecating face.

"Do you know her?" asked Mady. "I know her very well, she is 'well known'. You can go if you want too, it's up to you," she said, turning away and leaving a flabbergasted Mady, who didn't know wether it was worthwhile for him to visit the other Congress but he was definitely interested to meet the sexy Roxana again.

At 9 p.m. Mady met Roxana in the lobby of the Claridge. She was elegant, sexy, desirable, thought Mady. "Where shall we go now?" he asked her.

"I hear the restaurant here in the Claridge is quite good and it has just started to rain outside. Why couldn't we stay here?" she asked. Mady had no reason to object. It passed his mind that if they stayed in the hotel he could charge the evening's expenses to his hotel account.

The Claridge restaurant did not disappoint the couple. The meal and the desserts were excellent and they had the particular red wine Roxana asked for. Mady only realized how heavy the wine was when after an hour or so he started to feel dizzy and still hadn't embraced the subject of going to Roxana's meeting. There was a pianist playing but there was no dancing. Roxana laughed a lot and her eyes were particularly shining. Mady felt like kissing her.

At about 11 p.m., after they'd finished eating and drunk the bottle of red wine, Roxana suggested, "We could go up to your room and have a cognac there?" It was an excellent idea, Mady thought. They left the restaurant and he went to the reception to pick up his room keys. That was when disaster struck!

Instead of giving him the keys, the receptionist told him with a stern face: "You may not entertain female guests in your room in this hotel, Sir. I'm sorry."

Mady was shattered. What would he tell Roxana? Did the receptionist think she was a whore? While Mady felt so miserable that he couldn't move, Roxana, who heard the exchange, walked up to Mady, grabbed his arm and told him in front of the receptionist, "Come, I know another place where we can go."

With Roxana leading the way, they walked arm in arm on the well-worn pavement with slightly uncertain steps until Roxana pointed out a small hotel with the name "REX". "This is it," she said and pulled Mady in.

To Mady's surprise, when she asked the receptionist for the key to a single room, the man gave it to her without expressing any surprise. *Did he know her?* wondered Mady.

Roxana opened the door of a first floor room. The room was dark, lit only by the hotel's neon sign on the outside. Mady instinctively looked for a switch to turn the lights on but Roxana pushed him toward the single bed that seemed to him the only furniture in the room.

As Mady tried to look around, while he was dragged toward the bed, he fleetingly saw Roxana discarding first her shoes, then her pieces of clothing, the frock, the blouse, her camisole, her bra and her panties. She jumped onto the bedcover naked, pulling Mady on with outstretched arms. She kissed Mady hungrily but he was put off by the strong smell of wine on her mouth.

However nature took its way and within minutes they were locked together, moving like wrestlers. The only noise was their wild breathing and Roxana's occasional cries of "si, si".

Almost immediately, after ending the first stormy coupling, Roxana pulled herself on to Mady again and started to move wildly, which excited him and he joined in actively. There was no talk, neither said anything. Then they lay on their backs and Mady started thinking of how their relationship was going to develop after this episode, when with a sigh, Roxana suddenly grasped hold of his penis, thrust it inside her and started pumping him all over again.

After a while, Mady managed to satisfy Roxana's seemingly unlimited sexual desire but he decided to end his relationship with her. She was too hard to satisfy. Going to the other Congress, a move which was also connected with Roxana, looked dubious too. Thankfully, after the third time, both lovers were exhausted and they fell into a deep sleep.

At 3.30 a.m. Mady woke, got up, left the sleeping Roxana and walked back to his hotel. At 8 a.m. he was sound asleep when Schmidt woke him up and told him that Longo was kidnapped by the Tupamaros overnight and they left a note saying "You will be contacted". As Longo lived alone in his house, Mady didn't understand who they had in mind.

"Who will be contacted?" Mady asked. Schmidt wasn't any help. He seemed to be without any plan, any suggestion. "We'll just have to wait and see. I will send a report to Mr Leon Adler, of course, and wait for his instructions."

Schmidt continued: "You should stick to your regular program. Go to the Congress and after that, stay in the hotel so I can always find you. More importantly, the kidnappers might find you if you stay in the hotel."

"That's absurd!" burst out Mady. "What could they possibly want from me?"

"You never know. At this stage we are in the dark and just have to wait for their 'contact.' I will, of course, communicate with the Police and with Mr Leon Adler. Don't do anything foolish. This is a waiting game and the stakes are high. Do as I told you!" With this, Schmidt left.

Chapter X.

Saturday, at 10 a.m., Mady went to the Congress. Cabral was already waiting for him at their seats. "Longo was kidnapped by the Tupamaros!" he said by way of greeting.

"How do you know?" asked Mady. "The Chairman just announced it." *This is madness. I am the one learn it last but Schmidt thinks they may will contact me. Why me? What could I do? They say these kidnappings are always about money. Longo has no money as far as I know. All he has got are his house and his unpatented invention. How could he, or rather who would possibly suddenly get a lot of money? They said the Tupamaros asked for and received one million dollars for the FIAT President. If that's their regular fee, what is going to happen to Longo?*

As Mady was working out what he should do, if anything, suddenly Roxanna appeared and grabbed his arm.

"When shall we meet tonight?" she asked loudly, disregarding Cabral's surprised face. "I've got your official invitation to our Congress," she said, offering Mady a piece of paper.

"I am not going to your Congress and we cannot meet anymore," said Mady brusquely.

"What's wrong, Chico? Don't you like me anymore?" asked Roxanna, hanging onto Mady's arm.

"It's not that. I got a bad cold last night," said Mady and pulled his arm away from Roxanna's grip. He thought he couldn't handle more complications after Longo's kidnapping and the disciplinary action in Hungary.

"I haven't got a cold," she said, and as she turned away she added, "I will ring you."

She walked away with hips swinging, reminding Mady of his first and only South American sexual adventure.

The *Corriere della sera,* the afternoon paper, reported on its front page: DOCTOR GLAUCO LONGO, FAMOUS BIOCHEMIST, WAS KIDNAPPED BY THE TUPAMAROS WHO DEMAND ONE MILLION DOLLAR RANSOM.

Somebody brought in several copies of the paper to the Congress, where the ongoing presentation was interrupted and the Chairman read out the news. He also announced that for the rest of the day there would be no presentations. He formed an ad hoc committee with himself and the two Vice-Presidents to make a decision about what the Congress should do, under the circumstances.

Mady was woken up from his reveries when he heard his name. He had completely forgotten that he was one of the Vice-Presidents. He considered it just a polite gesture, an honorary position with no duties to perform, and now, he was in the middle of a typical South American chaos. *Well, I have to go. I'll just keep mum and say yes to whatever the others say,* he decided, when the Chairman invited him and Dr Joaqim Otto, the other Vice-President, into his office.

"Take a seat, gentlemen," Dr Bocchi said as he greeted the two Vice-Presidents. Coffee, or something stronger perhaps? No? Okay, lets get down to business. I'll tell you what I had in mind, then you can add your suggestions.

"First of all we, as a body of professional people, have to express our outrage and our condemnation of this lawless act, which casts a shadow on Argentina. We demand that the authorities act urgently and vigorously to free our colleague and remove the shadow that has been cast on all of us. No ideological tenet could justify such an act against humanity. The perpetrators have to be arrested and receive their just punishment. We demand this, on behalf of all peace loving people."

"Shouldn't we go straight to the police? After all it is their responsibility to free Dr Longo and bring the guilty ones to justice?" asked Dr Otto. *It is amazing, how many people of German extraction are in Argentina,* went trough Mady's mind.

"I think it would be sufficient to approach the problem the way Dr Bocchi proposed," said Mady. Then, as an afterthought, he asked, "What about the one million dollars they are asking for? Do we have any idea what happens if nobody comes up with the ransom money? Could the Government, the rich pharmaceutical companies, or private people, or charities come up with that kind of money? The way I understand it the Tupamaros have killed hostages before when they didn't get the money."

"The official attitude is that the government doesn't make deals with criminals. That would only encourage them in further criminal acts. We can just wait and hope that the authorities will do their job.

"As for the big companies, Pfizer, Merck, Hoechts, they have already contacted me to express their commiseration, but there is no question of them coming forward with money. Look at it this way, I believe that one million dollars is too much for any of them and they wouldn't pool their money together to help. They are competitors! They use their money only for investments! If we are in agreement, I'll put together our PR announcement for the papers. Thank you, and see you tomorrow."

Mady was happy that the unpleasant meeting was over. He didn't like Bocchi's expression that their communiqué was a PR, a public relation exercise. But what could he do? *Nothing*, he thought. He went back to his hotel, picked up a couple of sandwiches in the cafeteria and started for his room when the receptionist called out to him, "A lady is waiting for you in the lobby, sir."

Chapter XI.

THAT HAS TO BE Roxannna, he thought. *I have to get rid of that woman.* It wasn't Roxanna! An elegant, good-looking, blond woman was sitting in one of the lounge chairs. Mady didn't know her.

Still, there was nobody else there, so Mady approached her, saying, "I'm Dr Mady, are you waiting for me? I don't think we have met." He offered his hand but the woman, she could be 35 or 40, thought Mady, stood and said, "We have something confidential to discuss. Couldn't we go up to your room?" With this he picked up her handbag, ready to go.

Mady remembered the episode when he was told not to 'entertain' women in his room, so he stopped her. "It's not convenient at the moment," he said. "We could talk here, there is nobody else around." And with this he offered the woman one of the armchairs at a cafe table and he sat on another. Mady could tell that the visitor didn't like this change but she sat and now she offered her hand.

"Gisele Huper, from Swisswell in Zurich. I've heard a lot about you, Dr Mady. Good to meet you at last.

"Mr Leon Adler sent me to you. I've come in connection with the unfortunate case of Dr Longo, who happens to be my ex-husband."

Mady sighed deeply but said nothing. *This is the day of surprises,* he thought. He couldn't imagine the reason for Huper's visit. "What do you wish to discuss with me, Miss Huper?"

Huper looked around before she spoke; "What I'm telling you is strictly confidential and it could have dire consequences if it gets out. At this stage only you and I know about it. You understand?" Mady just nodded. He understood. No funny business with the Tupamaros.

"The one million dollars ransom is not the only problem," started Huper very quietly.

"Swisswell would provide the money. Nobody else would. It is a strange twist of fate that it is not the Tupamaros who are causing problems but the kidnapped man himself. The Tupamaros would accept Swisswell's money but Glauco, my idiotic ex, would not. Can you imagine such stubbornness?

"I cannot accept Glauco's idiotic refusal but knowing him I can follow his line of thinking," continued Huper. "He has spent year after year on producing 'Malantin', his wonder drug for eradicating malaria. He could have patented it already, if not for a bureaucratic mistake at the Patent Office which caused delays. In the meantime "Swisswell" managed to get their 'Antimal' patented. They may have bribed somebody at the Patent Office to hold back their rival's patent. Nobody will ever know.

"Swisswell is offering now to pay, under the veil of secrecy, the one million dollars ransom under two conditions; one, Glauco sells 'Malantin' to Swisswell with all documentation, and two, he undertakes not to conduct any more research into malaria.

"Does he refuse to accept Swisswell's conditions? He could be killed. The Tupamaros don't play fair!" Mady burst out.

"The reason for his refusal is that Swisswell already has the market for their 'Antimal'. If they get his 'Malantin' they will lock it up and the world will never know of his back-breaking, many years long work. He'd rather die, he says, than let Swisswell get their hands on the fruit of his greatest achievement."

"So what is the solution?" asked Mady. "We have the solution," answered Huper. "If it is played right, it can save that idiot's life and get 'Malantin' docked Make it disappear. Before we go any further, think hard. Have you ever told Glauco that you have any connection with Swisswell? This is very important. Have you?"

"No, I don't think so," answered Mady.

"Okay, then read this," said Huper and gave Mady a contract form, printed on a lawyer's business paper, signed by someone from 'Karpathia Medicine' and by the lawyer who set out the contract. There was space left for another signature, for Dr Glauco Longo. Mady had never heard of 'Karpathia Medicine' or of the lawyer. "What is this?" he asked confused.

"This is the solution!" exclaimed Huper. "If Longo signs this contract, the Tupamaros will get the one million dollars, Glauco will be freed and Swisswell will get Malantin.

"This sounds like a fairytale to me. How do you imagine this will work?"

"Let's have a coffee and I'll explain everything." With this Huper stood. "Maybe we could finish the details in your private room?"

"It's still not convenient, we can talk here undistured. They'll bring the coffee here," said Mady and showed Huper to the armchair, while he ran toward the cafeteria to order two coffees, cursing Claridge's 'no women' rule.

The waiter brought the two coffees and they chatted while they drank. The whole picture was a blur for Mady so he started to question Huper. "How did you get into this mess? Where are you staying in Buenos Aires? Have you, or anybody else had contact with your ex or with the Tupamaros?"

To all his questions he received the same polite answer with a smile; "No questions please. Just concentrate on what I'm telling you. I'll tell you everything that matters, what you have to know to fulfil your very important mission. Of course you will be well compensated for your troubles, but that will come later, so listen to what really matters now.

"'Karpathia Medicine' is a medium size company set up on a 50/50 basis by the Hungarian and the Romanian governments. Swisswell recently bought the company secretly by buying up all their shares. You, as a Hungarian doctor, are suitable to represent that company. Let's say the company wishes to make a significant investment in a new product. They hear about Longo's invention, so far unpatented, and they decide Malantin could be their big chance to break into the market. So they approach you, you happen to be going to Argentina on previous arrangement and this will save them your travelling expenses. Clear?"

Chapter XII.

- -

"How will I get into contact with Longo and the Tupamaros?"

"It is already arranged. I will take you there and the Tupamaros will organize your meeting with him. You will then tell that idiot, that he has to sign this contract, because this is his only chance to stay alive. Capisci?"

"What if he starts asking questions?"

"You tell him, 'no questions'! He will be taken care of. And another thing, he is not supposed to know that I had anything to do with this. Alright? Actually, best if nobody knows about me being here!"

They decided that Mady should still go to the last day of his Congress and to the closing banquet on Sunday evening, and that Gisele Huper would come to pick him up on Monday morning at the Claridge and take him to the 'secret meeting'.

There were only two presentations on the last morning. They were followed by an official closing ceremony, during which 'Certificates of attendance' were given to all delegates one by one, which took about two hours.

Mady had lunch alone in the Churrasco Restaurant, then went back to the Claridge and lay down to be fresh for the evening banquet in the ballroom of the Saint Martin hotel at 10 p.m. *Could this be true? Wondered Mady, starting a banquet at 10 p.m.? When will it end? I've had enough of Argentina,* he sighed, remembering that his problems might only start after the Congress.

After waking up from his afternoon nap, Mady had a shower and ate a couple of sandwiches he had stored in the small hotel refrigerator, keeping in mind that later at the banquet, he would obviously have some proper food. *I'm sure there will be enough meat, meat, meat,* he thought, wishing to get out of this Argentine circle of over-eating.

Mady walked to the Saint Martin hotel in the city and it was 9.45 p.m. when he asked the receptionist where in the hotel the Medical Congress banquet would be held. He was told that it would be on the top floor. Mady came deliberately early, before the 10 p.m. opening, expecting some confusion with the seating arrangements.

He took the elevator to the top floor where he found himself in an elegant lobby, with red wallpaper and gilded mirrors all around, but no people, who Mady expected to be there running around, organizing details of the evening.

Am I at the right place? he asked himself, looking around. He looked in through a wide door with glass sections and saw uniformed people running around, some with brooms, some carrying chairs, some making table settings.

It's almost opening time, this couldn't be the right place, he thought and kept knocking on the door, until one man passed by inside, carrying a chair, and asked what he wanted. "Is this the place for the Medical Congress ball?" "Yes it is," said the man and left, not waiting for any further inquiries.

This is Argentina for you, murmured Mady and sat down on a chair, waiting for the evening's events to unfold. It was past 10.30 p.m. when guests arrived, chatting loudly, and sat at their places marked by name cards. Mady thought that somebody he knew, like Cabral, or Bakos will be his neighbour, but had no such luck.

Long tables were set up in a U-form and there were, according to Mady's estimate, about 150 guests, mainly couples. President Bocchi sat at the middle table. He soon rose, greeted the guests and with a few words praised the work of the Congress. In reply, somebody Mady didn't know praised Bocchi's leadership and the work of the organizers. Everybody drank to that.

Next to Mady, at the end of the table, Mady's neighbours were a young couple who introduced themselves as Dr and Mrs Nussbaum. They were pleasant enough and Mady politely told them in a few words how much he had enjoyed the Congress and Buenos Aires. He added that he would leave in 48 hours and go back to Hungary.

"Oh, you are from Hungary?" asked Dr Nussbaum. "How is the Communist system working? The Jews are safe there, aren't they?"

"Of course, of course," answered Mady who was caught unprepared by the question and felt uncomfortable. *What could I speak about with these people?*

The Nussbaums solved Mady's problem by saying; "This is our last International Congress. Next month we are leaving, emigrating to Israel." Mady didn't want to get involved in discussing the reasons for Nussbaum's decision. He deliberately kept out of discussing anything in connection with the Jews in Hungary. *I have no problem with them*, he thought and that determined his attitude.

The ball ended after several noisy toasts, self gratulations and statements that "we shall meet again." It was well after midnight when Mady went to Bocchi to thank him for the invitation and expressed his hopes that there would be other similar congresses.

Chapter XIII.

MONDAY MORNING AT 9 a.m. - as agreed - Gisele Huper came to pick up Mady at the Claridge hotel. She left her car in front of the hotel and urged Mady, who was sitting in the lobby, to finish his coffee and get into the car, not to waste time. "I've brought hot coffee in a thermos and a few sandwiches. You won't die of hunger or thirst. We are going only for an hour or so.

"Here, take this folder. The contract Glauco has to sign is in the folder. It is in English. You'd better study it. You may have to read it to him." With this she gave Mady a blue folder, got into the car and switched on the engine.

Mady started to feel dizzy. *What is this rush and why would I have to read the contract to Longo? Can't he read? What have they done to him? What did I get myself into? Maybe I should just walk out and claim that I don't want to have anything to do with Longo's problem?*

Huper seemed to be aware of Mady's thoughts and possible change of heart because she suddenly said to him: "Naturally you will be well compensated for your troubles. I was authorized to tell you that you will receive 10,000 dollars as soon as this action is over."

Mady's first reaction was, *10,000 dollars, that's something!* but before he could feel really happy, he asked himself, *how could I have that sort of money without anybody knowing about it in Hungary? I cannot put it in the bank. Should I hide it somewhere, worrying all the time that it was not discovered? I don't know, I'll work out something, let's just get over this Longo part and cease contact with these people.*

Time passed quickly. They left the suburbs and started to drive on country roads. When they came to some deserted streets, Huper stopped the car. The area looked like a deserted village. Mady couldn't see any people or animals around.

Huper pointed to a small church in the distance. It was in a run-down state. "That's where you have to go. They've got Glauco there. They are waiting for you. Take the contract when you go. Don't you want to have a little coffee before going?" Huper was noticeably nervous.

I might as well have some coffee, told himself Mady, who felt his own nervousness rising. *No wonder, I've never been in a situation like this before. Maybe these Tupamaros, whoever they are, have some plan for me too? Who will save me, if I'm in trouble?*

"Let's get it over," he said loudly, got out of the car and started for the little church, holding the blue folder with the contract high.

The old timber door of the church opened with a loud creaking noise. At first glance Mady saw nobody inside. He stopped and looked around. Soon a figure in a long black coat, wearing a black ski mask, appeared from the background and pointed Mady toward the confessional box, then melted again into the background.

Mady walked to the confessional, opened the altar-side door and entered. The little cabin was divided. A grill covered the faces on both sides. Longo was sitting, tied to a chair on the other side. Only his right hand was free. *To be able to sign the contract,* assumed Mady.

He suddenly realized that Longo would be able to see his face! *I don't want that,* he reacted wildly and looked around, wondering, how to maintain his anonymity? *Real Argentine organizing talents,* he thought bitterly but then he saw a black ski mask hung on a nail, next to a small copper bell like the ones hotel receptionists had. *Obviously for me,* he thought, *but they forgot to tell me.* With this he put on the black mask that left only his eyes and his mouth open and turned toward Longo.

"I'm here to help you, Dr Longo," he started his improvised speech. Your captors want one million dollars for your release. A continental pharmaceutical firm is willing to pay them to have you freed, under some conditions. I have with me the contract for you to sign and as soon as your captors receive the agreed amount, they will free you."

Mady held up the contract for Longo to see. "Do you want me to read it to you, before you sign it, Dr Longo?" Mady felt very stupid as soon as he asked the question.

"Of course I want you to read it to me! What a stupid question," croaked Longo and his face expressed his anger.

"Alright, I'm reading it," said Mady, "but let me finish the reading, then you can comment on it if you wish, though I have to warn you that this is an unconditional offer! Not negotiable!" Mady read loudly the one page contract.

Longo had one question, "Why would they care if I would continue, or start a new research?" Mady half-expected this question but didn't want to enter any discussion with Longo. "No questions, please. I'm only a messenger. You can sign here and the sooner that's done, the faster you'll be with your son."

Mady didn't plan to say that and as soon as he said 'your son', he could have bitten off his tongue. *There goes my anonymity. Maybe he didn't catch on,* he wished and thought he should never tell about this slip-up to the Tupamaros. But it was too late!

"You're Dr Mady! I recognized you by your accent," cried out Longo and started to shake the ropes holding him down.

"Shut up! You are a fool. The only question is whether you sign and live, or you don't sign and you die here in this desert." With this Mady shook the small bell, his only communication with the world.

Within a couple of minutes the black coated man with the black ski mask opened the door. "Que passa?" he asked and faint signs of a foreign accent hit Mady's ears. He was worried about his own 'traitor' accent.

Mady also noticed that the man was wearing stout ankle boots. *When not in the city, locals wear riding boots,* went through Mady's mind. *Could this be Karl Schmidt, in a 'fake' Tupamaro kidnapping? No, that's too fantastic,* he told himself and tried to put the idea out of his mind.

"He'll sign now," said Mady to the visitor and gave the folder to the man to pass it on to Longo, get it signed and returned it to him. This act was completed in one minute without any further words from Longo.

Finally Longo understood the seriousness of his situation, sighed Mady. *Even though he might have recognized me, it is not leading him to Swisswell. Still, the sooner I get out of this country, the better it will be. Maybe the whole episode was just a bad dream, but what about my 10,000 dollars? Is that a dream too?*

After the black-coated man returned the signed contract to Mady, he signalled that he could go. Mady walked straight to Huper who waited in her car. She took the folder without a word, checked whether it was signed and without asking Mady for any details of his mission, started the car and took him back to the Claridge.

On their way back to the city, only one thing occupied Mady's mind. "How does he get the agreed money? Finally he couldn't wait any longer for Huper to bring up the question and he asked her. "How do I get the 10,000 dollars?"

"It is really up to you," answered Huper. "It has to be deposited for me outside Hungary," said Mady, who had heard about secret Swiss bank accounts.

"That's alright," agreed Huper. "How about a numbered secret account in the Bank of Zurich? You have to give me the numbers, of course. You can trust me," she said and took out a biro, looking expectantly at Mady.

After a short hesitation, Mady gave Huper his home phone number, 1104 52, which she wrote on the top of the folder. "When are you leaving?" Huper asked Mady.

"I have an Aerolineas Argentina ticket for tomorrow morning, booked by the Congress for me. And when are you leaving?" asked Mady politely.

"I don't know yet," was the answer.

Just before leaving the Claridge, Huper suddenly remembered something; "I nearly forgot. We have to sign the contract as witnesses to Longo's signature." With this she took the contract out of its folder and after a moment's hesitation signed it, then offered to Mady to sign it too, under her signature. Taking back the document Huper didn't get out of the car. She offered her hand to Mady through the side window and said, "hasta la vista," and drove away.

Chapter XIV.

MADY LEFT BUENOS AIRES on Tuesday morning and the Aerolineas Argentina took him back to Europe on the same route as he had come to Buenos Aires. In Zurich Mady had to change planes. After a five hour layover the Lufthansa plane was to take him back to Budapest.

Mady sent a telegram to his friend, Dr Laszlo Pinter, advising him of his arrival time. He wanted to find out from Pinter what was happening while he was away that concerned him.

While in Zurich, he had a problem about the promised 10,000 dollars that Swisswell was supposed to deposit into his numbered account in the Bank of Zurich. Will Swisswell keep their word? Should he make a short visit to the Bank to check if the money has been deposited to his name, or number, that is?

He had enough time before he had to join the Lufthansa connection, so why did he hesitate to visit the Bank? Mady confessed to himself that his main worry in connection with the Swisswell money was, *not to alert the Hungarian Communist government to the fact that the money existed and it was his 'Payment for service!'*

If they find out, my professional career is finished, he thought bitterly. *So what is the use of all that money, if it means only trouble for me? But after all, it is a tidy sum and I am the rightful owner. It would be idiotic to let it go to waste. I'd better not show myself at the bank before I work out what would be the best way to use it without taking any risk*, he decided.

In Budapest, at the Ferihegy airport, he had a surprise. His friend Pinter was there, but he was not alone. Anna, the assistant was waiting for Mady too. *What is this? Why would Anna wait for me? Anna, who allegedly acted against me at the Ministry?* Pinter embraced Mady, then Anna kissed him.

"Let's have an espresso. They have good coffee here," suggested Anna. With this, she took Mady's arm and pulled him toward the cafeteria. Mady looked at Pinter to see his reaction to this, after all it was Pinter who warned Mady in the telegram about Anna. Mady looked questioningly at Pinter to see his reaction. Nothing! Pinter just followed the couple without saying a word.

Once they were sitting, waiting for their espressos, Mady couldn't keep quiet about his problem, allegedly started by Anna. "So what is happening in my 'disciplinary case' in the Ministry, Anna?" he asked her.

Before Anna could open her mouth Pinter intervened. "Not here, not now, not in my presence! I know the whole story from Anna. I was wrong suggesting that it was of her making. Go home with Anna and let her explain what exactly has happened," Pinter took his hat and left without drinking his coffee.

"Is this alright with you? Will you come with me and clear up this 'mystery'?" asked Mady. Anna just nodded and stood to go. She had her small FIAT car in the parking lot. Mady put in his single suitcase and they left the airport for Mady's flat in Kristof Square in the city.

Mady had his flat, which included his private surgery, on the first floor of an old, elegant apartment house. Mady's professional life was arranged the way most other doctors lived and worked under the Communist government. He had to be on call at least two days every week at a public clinic, or hospital. That gave him the right to conduct a private practice on the other days in his speciality.

Mady's specialities were gynaecology, sexually transmitted and infectious diseases. His few private patients were mainly those who for various reasons didn't want to visit the public clinics. He usually had two or three patients a day in his private surgery, where the dining room became the waiting room and one of the bedrooms became the surgery. Anna assisted him both in the Kutvolgyi Clinic and in his home surgery.

In the Kutvolgyi Clinic the patients were mainly Communist Party and government officials and their relatives. Some of those became his private patients too.

When they arrived at Mady's flat, they sat in the waiting room. Without further ado Mady asked Anna; "Tell me what is happening that concerns me and what was your role in it?"

"The whole business was stirred up by Mrs Bartha, the wife of the Secretary of State for the Interior. Do you remember her?" Mady just shook his head in answer. "Anyway," continued Anna, "Mrs Bartha lodged a complaint at the Disciplinary Committee of the Ministry, claiming that you attacked her sexually when she was your patient."

"Excuse me, excuse me," interrupted Mady. "What in the hell has the Ministry for the Interior got to do with me?"

"Well, that's not the strangest part. Administratively you are on the Ministry's payroll, in Group V., like the Captains of the Police, so technically they could handle her complaint if it came to that.

"Now, let me describe the whole sordid picture,". continued Anna. "Mrs Bartha visited the Kutvolgyi Clinic before you left for Switzerland. She came for a regular 'Pap smear test'. I can still remember that she was on Dr Klara Revesz's list but before she was called in, she asked the receptionist to be treated by you instead of the woman doctor.

The receptionist complied – remember she is the wife of the Secretary of State - and she came to us. I remember her because she behaved provocatively, wore tiny red panties and asked many questions after you did the smear test. It was hard to get her out of the surgery. I distinctly remember that before she left she asked me for your private phone number and address."

"Did I see her again, privately?" asked Mady.

"No, and that's the funny part," said Anna. She asked for me on the phone in the clinic and asked when could she see you? I told her you were in Switzerland. Sometime later she phoned again and I told her that you were in Argentina attending a congress. It was not a secret. She started shouting on the phone, saying, "For whom is he working? Who pays his wages? The Swiss? The Argentines?"

"After her outburst, she sent a letter to the Ministry, accusing you of working for the Swiss and neglecting your patients here. She also added that you behaved unethically when you examined her in your private surgery."

"What happened then?" asked Mady.

"Well, the whole thing died down before you returned. I was called in to the Ministry and questioned about Mrs Bartha's allegations. When I told them that the woman had never visited you privately and that your two trips were approved by the government they dropped all actions and told me to treat the case confidentially, not to tell anyone about it, including you. So you should keep mum about the whole Mrs Bartha business too, or I could get into trouble. Alright? Kiss me and forget about the whole episode."

Anna went up to Mady and planted a long kiss on his lips. "Let's have a cognac," he suggested as soon as he regained his breath. He took out a bottle of cognac and two balloon glasses and led Anna into the bedroom. "It's warmer here," he said. He put down the glasses on the bedside table. Anna kicked off her shoes and sat on the bed.

After tasting the cognac, Anna moved to Mady, kissed and embraced him. "I love you Andrew," she whispered. Mady returned the kiss and leaned back on the bed pulling Anna with him. Getting rid of their street clothing took only a few seconds. Their love making was stormy, passionate. With short intervals, mainly to regain their breath, they repeated their embrace two more times. "I love you, I love you," repeated Anna numerous times, which Andrew returned by saying, "I love you too."

Mady's brain didn't switch off during their love making. *No woman loved me this much, what was I waiting for? How will this affair end?* circulated in his mind.

Chapter XV.

THE END OF THE Longo saga was played out after Huper and Mady left.

Longo kept pulling on his ropes impotently when the masked man opened the cubicle and left the door open.

"Finally you came to your right mind, Dr Longo. You only have to follow the conditions set for you and you can continue your normal life. You are in San Lorenzo, a place 60 km from Buenos Aires. There are no inhabitants, no telephone, no transport from here. It has been deserted since the last earthquake about 40 years ago. You will be free to go after I leave. You can walk on a track from here to the Buenos Aires highway by about 15 km. from here. There is traffic there, cars, trucks, buses.

"Now, about the conditions. Do not contact the police, don't give newspaper interviews about your 'adventure', don't talk negatively about the Tupamaros. They wouldn't like that and they could be very angry. You know what that could mean? Understood?" Longo just nodded and said "si".

During the masked man's long speech Longo was thinking feverishly; *His accent, I've heard that accent before, it's similar to Gisele's German accented Spanish, but not quite the same. Could it be Swiss-Dutch? Neither Dr Mady, nor this man, are Tupamaros. The Tupamaros speak their native Spanish, they are from Uruguay. But who are they?* Then he realized that the man was watching him, watching his reaction to the conditions he was just told. *First I just have to get out of this hellhole, then I will have time to make decisions.* "Io comprendo," he told the man and nodded.

"Mui bueno," said the man and moved to loosen Longo's ropes, but didn't free him completely. "You can get rid of the rest," he said and left.

In the last minute he turned and added, "We are still watching you. Best for you not to leave the place in less than an hour."

Longo slowly, cautiously moved to loosen the ropes and in what seemed to him an eternity, he found he could stand up. First he massaged his limbs which had gone into cramps from the long rigid posture. Then he looked out of the cabin. He saw nothing but a deserted field, wind chasing the sand and dry leaves. *I might as well start going toward the highway. I should get there before dark, if the man was not lying about the distance from here.*

Longo reached the Highway before dark and managed to flag down a tourist bus, telling the driver that his car had broken down. At his request the bus stopped for him about three corners from his Villa Ballester house. The house was closed down, as he expected, but he found the spare key he hid in a concrete flower vase at the back. He opened the house and when he smelled the well-known odours, he thought, *I was never happier in my life then now, here, back in my own house.* He lay down and fell into a deep sleep.

The phone woke Longo at 9 a.m. the next day. After a moment of hesitation, he answered it. "Pronto, Papa, is it you?" said the caller.

"Edoardo, is it you?" asked Longo, who was still sleepy, but he was happy to hear his son's voice.

"Have you seen the morning edition of the *PRENSA* papa? They say you were not kidnapped by the Tupamaros. The same paper wrote two days ago that you were. What happened, Papa? I tried to call you yesterday, but there was no answer."

"I went for a bus tour with colleagues to clear my head from all the scientific stuff I heard at the Congress," said Longo, using the first explanation that came to his mind. "Would you believe it the bus broke down in the middle of nowhere. There was no electricity, no phones in the area. The driver had to walk a long distance to find a phone. In the meantime it got dark and we had to sleep in the bus. Help came only in the morning and they brought us back. So much about the Tupamaros story. By the way when can I see you?"

"Not before Christmas. There is no way I can get away from the Academy before that. I'm happy to hear you are well," said Edoardo and promised to ring again before Christmas.

Chapter XVI.

--- -- -- -- - -- -- -- -- - -- -- -- - -- - --

LONGO WARNED HIMSELF TO stay calm while working out a plan of action which would clear up what really had happened and who was behind it. He was determined to make invalid the contract he was forced to sign. *I shouldn't make a noise about it, but engage a trustworthy lawyer,* he decided. *If there is public discussion, or police action, my enemies may try to silence me forever.*

The name of the lawyer Victor Rodriguez came to his mind, the lawyer who acted successfully in the FIAT kidnapping case.

I will approach Rodriguez, but first I have to get a copy of the PRENSA to see what has been said about me so far. Before he left for the city, Longo phoned Rodriguez for an urgent appointment and was given one for the same afternoon.

Rodriguez received Longo in his elegant office in the Florida and immediately surprised him by saying, "I was expecting you, Doctor."

"What do you mean you were expecting me? Even this morning, I myself didn't know that I would call you," said a surprised Longo, who was holding a copy of the *PRENSA* in his hand.

"I read the paper," said Rodriguez, pointing to the paper Longo was holding, and after reading the two contradictory stories in two days, I thought sooner or later you would come to me for help. Now that you are here, let's get down to business. First of all, let's start by you telling me exactly what happened to you in the last two days," said the lawyer and switched on a recorder.

Longo told Rodriguez everything that had happened from the moment when he was kidnapped by two masked men from his home, until he was released from the church in the desert.

"It is a strange story, particularly the signing of the contract with 'Karpathia Medicine'. Have you ever heard about that company? No? Since it seems that they are the beneficiaries of that contract, first we have to find out who are they and what are they doing. Of course that contract extracted from you under duress has no legal power but for a while let's just keep everything quiet, not to give them any excuse for further action. They don't seem to worry about legal consequences.

"Okay. Leave everything with me. See you in two days. As for you, you should go around, show people that you are alright and don't get into discussions about what has happened to you. Tell everybody that you didn't feel well for two days. Okay? As for finances, don't worry about it. We'll talk about that later."

After some hesitation Longo phoned Bocchi, the President of the already closed down Congress, and told him that he had been sick for two days and only today learned from the newspaper the 'fantasy story' about his kidnapping. Longo didn't think it was necessary to phone other colleagues to show that he was alright. *Bocchi is a gossip-monger, he will do that for me,* he thought and went to the Churrasco restaurant to have his first decent meal in two days.

After two days Longo went to see Rodriguez who seemed to be in a very good mood. "I thought straightaway that your kidnappers must have been amateurs. The way they acted told me that. Now we know for sure that they were amateurs indeed. Listen to this:

"The Karpathia Medicine company doesn't exist. Their address is a Bucharest post office number in Romania. A Swiss company, Swisswell, bought the Karpathia Medicine name a few months ago. You must have heard of Swisswell, I'm sure."

"I sure have. In the back of my mind I suspected them to be behind the 'kidnapping,'" said Longo and told Rodriguez about the foreign accents of the Hungarian Dr Mady and of the masked man's suspected Swiss-Dutch accent.

"Why didn't you tell me immediately?" asked the lawyer. "I didn't want to start you off in a wrong direction," answered Longo. "What will be our next step, Dr Rodriguez?"

"As I told you, the contract they exacted from you under duress is not legally binding, but that's not all. They would be lucky to escape with paying you a large sum of compensation for 'mental and physical suffering'. I'm talking about many millions of dollars!

"They will be reminded that kidnapping is punished with a jail sentence for life in Argentina! Now let's see, who will be our witnesses? If we keep on working on the quiet, that Hungarian doctor would not be likely to disappear but to get a Swiss witness will be more complicated. I will need time to work out that part of our strategy. Leave this with me. In the meantime, don't do anything to draw attention to yourself. I will call you when I need you," finished Rodriguez and offered his hand to Longo.

Chapter XVII.

In Lausanne, Mr Lafarge had a phone call from Albert Holzinger of the Swiss Intelligence organization, who wanted to meet him.

As soon as they sat in Lafarge's office, Holzinger started out on the business. "I had a call from our contact in the Bucharest Trademarks Office. He told me that a lawyer called Rodriguez from Buenos Aires made inquiries about Karpathia Medicine and subsequently about Swisswell. I suppose this inquiry has to do with the Glauco Longo patent application which we managed to hold back. Do you agree? What do you suggest we should do now?"

"As you know, Mr Holzinger, Longo has signed a contract with Karpathia Medicine with our 'help'. I suppose Longo's representative will attempt to prove the contract invalid and might try to start a counter-claim for damages. What do you think?"

"I agree," said Holzinger and added, "I'm sure that you don't want to face an Argentine tribunal in this matter. The question is how to prevent that happening."

"Let me check our data on the matter," said Lafarge and looked around for the file. After reading it he summarized it: "The way I see it, everything depends on who their witnesses could be and how we might counteract them with our witnesses."

Lafarge continued: "Let's see who has any direct knowledge of what happened to Longo. According to this report they are: Gisele Huper, Longo's ex-wife and our employee, your man Karl Schmidt, and a Hungarian doctor, Andrew Mady, who happened to be in Buenos Aires at the time. This Dr Mady was paid 10,000 dollars to try to convince, or otherwise persuade, Longo to sell his invention. There was also a

Brazilian doctor named Cabral from Rio de Janeiro but he was only an occasional contact of Longo, who also attended the Congress. These are the people we have to deal with, turning them into our witnesses for Longo's signing the contract voluntarily, at his own home," said Lafarge.

"I agree," said Holzinger, "but I have to make it clear that Karl Schmidt, a professional intelligence officer, cannot act publicly as a witness, so let's see what we can do with the others."

"Gisele Huper should be no problem," said Lafarge. "I will speak to her personally. The Hungarian doctor is a completely different case, though we have a handle on him. He'll probably agree to a reasonable suggestion as long as he doesn't get unmasked in front of the Hungarian Communist government as acting for us 'for money'."

"Well then, let's agree that I keep an eye on the Rodriguez-Longo duo. I don't think they will be moving very fast. You speak to Huper and maybe we'll discuss what to do and what to say to that Hungarian doctor. You already have a relationship with him and your visit to Hungary doesn't have to cause any upset with the government. Alright?" They agreed to keep in touch and Holzinger left.

Mr Lafarge didn't think he would have difficulty persuading Gisele Huper to act for Swisswell and against Longo's interest. After all, she had no objection when Lafarge commissioned her for the 'Tupamaro kidnapping action'. He knew there was no love lost between the couple and decided to mention to her that if Longo won a court case against Swisswell it would be at the price of implicating her in a crime, the 'kidnapping' in Argentina.

He would also express his and the company's gratitude to Gisele and promise to promote her to be Chief Researcher at Swisswell at a higher salary. Details of what she was expected to do would be spelled out later, after Holzinger returned with detailed plans.

A week later Holzinger asked for a meeting with Lafarge. In Lafarge's office they sat down to discuss details of what each one had to do. "As I suspected," started Holzinger, "Rodriguez first had a discussion with the police, then asked for a date with the Argentine Prosecutor General to begin the court case they are aiming for. Though something had sneaked out of Longo's false kidnapping case, so far Longo and Rodriguez refused to speak to the newspapers.

"Of course they are planning to cite Gisele Huper and Andrew Mady as their main witnesses for the 'duress' applied to Longo and threats to his life in case he refused to sign the prepared contract. Naturally, Huper and Mady being foreign citizens, not living in Argentine, not even having properties or other interests there, legally they are not obliged to appear before Argentine courts, not even to acknowledge the case against them. The only negative consequences for them would be not being able to travel to Argentine in the future.

Holzinger asked to see the contract. "I want to check the date on it. It is important to stick to that date. We must have proof that Huper and Mady were in Buenos Aires on that date, because we claim that's the date when those two visited Longo's house and were shown the signed contract by Longo. Best would be if you gave me a copy of the contract," said Holzinger and Lafarge made a copy for him in the office.

Chapter XVIII.

WITHIN ONE WEEK HUPER and Mady received letters from the Argentine consulates in Lausanne and in Budapest advising them that on a certain date they were expected to appear in front of a Buenos Aires court to testify about their role in the Glauco Longo kidnapping case. The registered letters required acknowledgement.

On Holzinger's advice, both declined to travel to Argentina. Gisele Huper offered to appear at the Lausanne Argentine consulate with her lawyer and make a deposition, while Mady offered to supply a written testimony made in the presence of a Hungarian Justice of Peace. Both requested to be supplied with any legal documents they were requested to answer to, before they gave their testimony. They also insisted on their contact with the Argentine authorities being kept confidential as a condition of their participation.

No further contact was made with them by the Argentine consulates before Christmas. The Catholic Argentine departments were closed down for a fortnight.

Gisele Huper was asked to appear at the Consulate in Lausanne on the 14th January. After discussing the request with Lafarge, she went to the consulate with the Attorney of the Swisswell company, Mr Klein. As soon as they entered the waiting room of the consulate Huper had the biggest surprise of her life.

A good-looking young man in an Argentine Naval Cadet uniform jumped up, came over to her and called out, "Mama!" It was Edoardo whom Gisele hadn't seen for years and the last time they met he was a skinny little boy. Mother and son embraced and kissed, then stood for a while speechless.

"Did your father send you to me?" asked Gisele. "Did he send you with a suggestion how to solve this tragic situation?"

"I wanted to come myself and told Papa about it. I am a man now and I couldn't stay uninvolved when the two people I love most in the world are trying to destroy each other's lives. Could we speak alone?" asked Edoardo and the lawyer who had heard all this left the room.

At his mother's prompting Edoardo spoke about the problems as his father explained it to him. "Papa is willing to stop his legal case against Swisswell, Karpathia Medicine and everybody involved in the 'hoax' kidnapping case, provided Swisswell will officially annul the 'bogus contract', declaring that it will not - it can not - serve as an obstacle to Papa's future work as a medical researcher. Naturally you yourself will have to refuse to act any further in any capacity, for Swisswell in the 'Longo case'."

"And these conditions will guarantee normal life for both of us?" asked his mother with tears in her eyes. "I love you, my son," she said, unable to see clearly, overwhelmed by her emotions as she held her son in her arms for the first time after many years.

"I think these conditions would suit both of you. Swisswell should not be inclined to be angry with you since they already have their antimalaria product patented and marketed all over the world, and Papa says he could use the fruits of his research by changing certain section to make it an 'anti-tse-tse fly' drug for Africa. Maybe we could be a family once again, mother?"

Fighting her tears, Gisele kissed her big son again and nodded. "Maybe we could," she agreed. With this she called back her lawyer and asked him to advise the Consul that Gisele Huper will not be available to make any statement in the 'Longo' case. Mother and son left the consulate together and went to Huper's house to talk about their past and future together.

Dr Andrew Mady received a very short phone call at his home from Switzerland.

"Case concluded, do not make any statements. You'll receive detailed explanation soon."

He was completely confused and his only thought was that he had to discuss his situation with somebody he could trust. Laszlo Pinter, Mady's only close friend came to mind and he called him for an important discussion.

Pinter came the same evening and Mady told him everything that happened in Argentina and since his return, the 'kidnapping', his own 'shameful role' in it, about the 10,000 dollars in the Bank of Zurich and the last piece of the puzzle, the phone call he just received telling him to stop any further action.

"What do you think, Laszlo?" "First of all I need a double cherry brandy. That's what I think. About your own role, after what you told me, I think you were crazy to get involved in this case but you are also lucky to get out of it. So what is left to think about? The 10,000 dollars?

"You are even more crazy if you are considering getting your hands on that money. The government would find out and that would be the end of Dr Andrew Mady, Hungarian medical practitioner. Send a telegram to the Bank of Zurich and instruct them to dispose of the 10,000 dollars by donating it to the University of Zurich Medical Faculty, anonymously. Capisci?"

"And you think that will be the end of the whole story? I have nothing else to do?"

"What more you could do, my friend? Get drunk and oh yes, screw Anna, who can hardly wait for you, and keep on screwing her until you both faint. That's my professional medical advice!" said Pinter and left.

Yankee Reunion In
London.

KATHLEEN FOREST, SECRETARY TO the US Secretary of Defence, wanted to go to the races on her first day in London. Russell Clark knew of her passion for gambling and quickly agreed. He had pangs of conscience for not writing to his fiancee since his appointment as Second Secretary to the American Embassy for almost a year. It was 6 p.m. when the pair got back to Russell's apartment after the Newmarket races.

Russell went to great length to create the right atmosphere for Kathleen's first visit in his Grosvenor Square apartment. He bought her favourite flowers, her favourite wine, choice cold snacks in aspic and Beluga caviar. Her favourite records were stacked on the turntable.

Kathleen walked to the windows and parted the curtains. Looking over the dark Grosvenor Square, she could see the huge metal eagle on the top of the American Embassy building and the illuminated outlines of the top and ground floors.

Russell followed her, hugged her and took off her coat. "It is dark. You can't see a thing. You'll be able to see the view in the morning," he said.

"Will I?" said Kathleen in a sultry voice, then turned and looked around, appraising the medium sized apartment. It was furnished with modern Scandinavian furniture which did not go well with the Georgian style of the building, she thought.

"My drink?" she asked, raising her eyebrows.

"Yes dear, coming right up," Russell humoured her. He had prepared the Brandy Alexander before leaving for the races. She put the tip of her tongue in the glass. "Umm, not bad," she said finally and reclined on the sofa holding her drink.

Russell switched on the record player, drank from his Chivas Regal and joined Kathleen on the sofa.

"To our reunion. Bottoms up," he proposed, then took the empty glasses to the small fold-down bar.

He returned to the sofa but did not sit down. Standing behind Kathleen he stroked her hair lightly, long enough to make Kathleen wonder what he was waiting for. Then he bent down, turned her head gently and kissed her mouth.

Still kissing her mouth, he stroked her neck, her shoulder and finally her breasts through the thin silk blouse. Her breathing became faster. She put her arms around his neck.

Russell felt hot. He wanted her very much. He knew he could have her but also knew that he could spoil the occasion by rushing her. They were experienced lovers. They knew each other's weaknesses and desires. Russell had to be patient and attentive if he wanted to get Kathleen in 'top mood'.

Standing behind the sofa he unbuttoned her blouse and fondled her breasts. Kathleen slowly opened her mouth to his exploring tongue. The tips of their tongues gently licked the inside of their lips and caressed each other in their own love affair.

"Why don't we slip into something more comfortable?" asked Russell, nodding toward the bedroom.

"You are getting lazy, lover," said Kathleen teasing him. She stood, straightened her blouse and went into the bedroom. Russell heard her going into the adjoining bathroom so he went into the bedroom himself. He pulled off the bedspread and waited. When he heard Kathleen taking a shower, he undressed. *Lucky, the central heating is working well,* he thought.

After a while Kathleen walked in, leaving the bathroom door open and the lights still on. Russell couldn't see her face, only the silhouette of her body. Russell admired her long legs and slender body. *She has a perfect figure,* he thought. *She looks taller than her five foot six inches.*

Kathleen lay on the bed naked, lying on her back. She didn't say a word.

"I love you, Kathy. You are beautiful," said Russell, pulling to her side, kissing her hair, her face.

"If you really love me why didn't you write? Why did I have to come to you?"

"I love you very much," said Russell. He embraced her and pulled her closer. His excitement was obvious and she was aroused too.

"Show me how much you love me," she said and closed her eyes.

Kathleen is beautiful. She hasn't changed. She still has the body of an eighteen-year-old. I don't think she'd ever want to risk this perfect body by having children, Russell told himself.

He knew that he would have to earn the pleasures Kathleen would give him by arousing her methodically, not leaving any part of her beautiful body untouched.

He pulled himself up on her side and stroked her hair and neck gently while kissing her lips. He kissed her upper lip, her lower lip, the corners of her mouth and her chin. He caressed her neck, her face, her breasts.

She kissed him back, and hugged him tight. Russell slid down, kissed her breasts, stroked her hips and her flat belly. She trembled when he kissed her belly-button. He then started to stroke her thighs.

Kathleen's thighs were closed. Russell lovingly admired, stroked and kissed her dense, soft hair that formed a perfect triangle. Her thighs slightly parted.

Russell started to kiss her toes, her feet and worked his way up kissing the inside of her legs, knees and her thighs gently pulling, stroking them apart just enough so that he could first stroke then kiss the inside of her thighs, the baby-soft skin-folds where the thighs parted. He felt the gentle rolling movements of her body and heard her heavy breathing. He straightened, embraced her tightly and kissed her passionately, trusting his erect part between her thighs. Kathleen helped him to roll on top of her and parted her legs to receive him.

Next morning the weather was unusually bright in London. Standing at the window in Russell's pyjamas, Kathleen drank her coffee slowly. Her eyes swept over the crowns of the old plane-trees covering Grosvenor Square. At the opposite end of the Square, the eagle on the top of the American Embassy seemed to be ready to take off to circle the Square. Bathing in the golden rays of the sun Kathleen felt good.

"Alright, I forgive you, but watch out! Washington is full of men who would be happy to entertain me," she said to Russell with an ominous warning.

A Ray Of Hope.
(Ireland - Australia)

TERRY CASEY, 20 YEAR old IRA soldier from Limerick, Ireland, suffered grave injuries to his head when he took part in a bombing attack against the Loughhall Ulster Constabulary (RUC) station on the 7th May 1987.

Eight members of the IRA Tyrone Brigade were gunned down by the British Special Air Services (SAS) and Terry was arrested. Terry's girlfriend, Moira O'Dea managed to escape and went underground under an assumed name. She continued her fight against the British, as a member of the reorganized Tyrone Brigade.

Terry lost his left eye and his right eye was damaged. He had a deep scar on his left cheek. Terry was treated in the hospital inside the MAZE prison, where all other IRA prisoners were kept in the B-Block.

Because of his condition, the authorities could not put Terry on trial for five months. Two days before the date set for his trial Terry was sprung by the IRA during a daring prison outbreak.

IRA experts falsified documents in the name of O'Hara, Terry's mother's name, and shipped him to Australia to his mother's aunt and uncle, the O'Haras, in the small West Australian town of Onslow.

Terry wore a black eye patch to cover the socket of his left eye. The long scar on his left cheek ended under the eye patch. After a few months his right eye healed to the point where he could read.

Moira learned of Terry's Australian address through her IRA contacts and wrote to him regularly under various names. He could not write to her for security reasons.

Five years passed and Terry's eyesight in his remaining right eye became gradually so bad that he couldn't read anymore. He was stuck without hope for a normal life in the small town of Onslow, which was

20 Km from the Australian Submarine Base in the Exmouth Gulf. His aunt and uncle took care of his physical well-being but he avoided and missed social contacts, clinging to the radio for news around the world and to Moira's letters. She was writing about "a victory in sight" and "their reunion in Ireland". Terry was tortured by a grave dilemma. *Has he got the right to shackle Moira to a blind man, or should he let her go?*

Patricia Kearney, a 28-year-old woman with an eight-year-old girl, came to the O'Haras almost every day, to help old Mrs O'Hara or to borrow something and chat with Terry. She was living next door, since her husband walked out on her.

One day the O'Haras drove to Port Headland. On their return there was a sand storm and a semi-trailer crashed into their car, killing them. Patricia came along with the police officer who told Terry what had happened.

In the O'Hara's will Terry inherited the house. Patricia offered to keep the house in order for him. When Terry became an Australian citizen he received an invalid pension from the Australian Government and some pension from the IRA too.

Patricia picked up Moira's letters from the local Post Office cum delicatessen shop and read them to Terry. She felt for him and was doing her best to soothe him when he talked about his doubts about what he should do when he returned to Ireland and met Moira again.

Moira's letters came under various names and this attracted the attention of the inquisitive postmistress, the interfering gossip, Heather Longbottom.

Moira wrote at least every two months. Patricia knew her name from Terry. When there was a mix up and the IRA killed two lawyers in Amsterdam by mistake, the newspapers described an unidentified girl who was also killed in the action. When there was no letter for three months, Patricia realized that probably Terry's Moira was the girl killed.

Terry was getting desperate and depressed as months went by without a letter from Moira. Patricia was fighting her own doubts, what to tell Terry, what to do to calm him. Terry became part of her life. She was thinking of selling her house, moving in with Terry and using the money from the sale to take Terry to Sydney, or the USA, for an operation to restore the sight in his right eye.

Finally she decided to write the 'Moira letters' herself, writing in them about IRA news she heard on television, describing her own feelings for Terry in Moira's name.

To keep on receiving overseas mail, Patricia wrote to overseas addresses she picked from advertisements in newspapers and magazines, who could be expected to answer a query from Australia. She replaced the answers in the original envelopes with letters of her own, written in Moira's name.

After a number of letters, Terry noticed changes in the style and first he tortured himself by imagining changes in Moira's feelings toward him. Later he recognized expressions and thoughts identical to ones he heard from Patricia. He angrily confronted Patricia and demanded an explanation.

Terry learned that Moira was dead and understood that Patricia loved him. He realized that Patricia and her daughter had become his family, his whole world and that Moira was only a romantic memory he clung to, the memory of his idealized youth.

Patricia convinced Terry that he should have the operation on his right eye. After getting the necessary referrals, they travelled to Sydney, where doctors at the Eye Clinic operated on him.

While they were away, Heather Longbottom secretly opened an overseas letter for Terry and found a handgun catalogue in it. She convinced herself that the strange couple were dangerous to the Onslow community, maybe even for the security of Australia. She reported her suspicions to the town's only police, Constable Pickles, who seized on it, as a possible chance for his promotion and his transfer to the 'city-lights' of Port Headland.

Constable Pickle's report was passed on to ASIO and Naval Intelligence at the Exmouth Naval Base. A small force of counter-intelligence agents were waiting for Terry and Patricia who were jubilantly returning after the successful operation which had restored Terry's eyesight.

Terry's case was cleared up when Patricia presented the collected letters and envelopes. Terry's IRA past was irrelevant on account of the years that had passed and because of moves afoot to end the Northern Ireland conflict permanently.

Roger's Christmas.
(Sydney)

THE NIGHT BEFORE CHRISTMAS Roger was at home in his Sydney flat. He'd finished working at four in the afternoon, parked his cab and gone home to have a rest. He slept till seven.

Though Christmas had no great religious significance for Roger, the festive face of the city, the colourful shop-windows, the hustle and bustle of the late shoppers had their effect on him. His thoughts went back to Christmases he spent as a child in his native Hungary and after the war in refugee camps for three years in France, before he came to Australia.

For a while he listened to his favourite opera, Verdi's Aida, but became restless, and decided to look for company.

Around 9 o'clock Roger entered the 'Flicks' espresso on Oxford Street, next to the Academy Twin Cinema. The place was full but he found a small table with one chair available. Pictures of film stars on the walls and canvas-backed collapsible chairs with famous directors' names on the back, cultivated the arty atmosphere which the owners and patrons aspired to.

Two women in their late twenties sat next to Roger at the next table. One had long straight hair, the other had the tousled 'after shower look' of Nicole Kidman. They were smoking and chatting and from time to time they looked around. Their off-handed, flippant expressions and postures suggested to Roger – who considered himself an expert in these sort of matters - that they were looking for company.

Never one to hesitate, Roger addressed the women: "Could I order drinks for you, mademoiselles?"

Without showing surprise, or apprehension, the 'mademoiselles' accepted the offer and Roger introduced himself as "Roger Corda, art photographer". The woman with the straight long hair was Linda, the tousled haired one was Noni. As soon as they drank up, Noni announced that she had to go and left the couple to their vices.

Linda gave the required opening to Roger by asking what sort of art photography he was doing. Roger rolled off his much used story about doing commissioned photos for magazines and portfolio pictures for models.

"You have a terrific photogenic face, Linda. I noticed it as soon as I saw you," he added and ordered further drinks.

"You are wrong about that," she said with a rueful smile. "I tear up most of my pictures. I look terrible in photos."

"Excuse moi, ma chere Linda, this is my profession. Your face-lines, facial bone structure and posture are as good as any professional model I ever saw." He finished his drink and as an afterthought he added, "I tell you what. Come with me and I'll prove it to you. I'll take a few pictures. You can see them in an hour. It doesn't cost you anything. It is my pleasure. I am happy to work with new, exciting models. My studio flat is just around the corner."

"I couldn't accept that," offered Linda weakly. "Your time and expenses..."

Roger got up, paid the bill and urged Linda to come along by pulling her chair back. She stubbed out her cigarette and stood. "Okay, if you think so," she said and straightened her black tricot top and red miniskirt.

Roger knew that his pad was not impressive so he pointed out the salient aspects of the place as he ushered Linda into his first floor walk-up flat. "I wanted to move to a more modern apartment many times, but this is so convenient. There are no neighbours to complain when I play my music loud and I love music, as you can see." He pointed to the shelves covering one wall with video cassettes and compact disks.

He picked up clothing left on chairs and on the sofa and took them into the bedroom. He smoothed the bed cover carefully, planning to get Linda on that bed soon.

"Drinks? Johnny Walker, cognac, vodka, something sweet or perhaps a long cold drink?"

"A screwdriver?" asked Linda.

"One screwdriver coming up," enthused Roger. "The ice and orange juice are in the kitchen, I'll be right back."

As he went to the kitchen, he left the door open and did not switch on the light in the corridor. He looked back to see what Linda was doing. Linda went to the shelves and Roger saw her sinking a few CDs in her bag.

Roger was neither surprised, nor upset. He was willing to pay for his pleasures and thought the CDs would be fair payment for laying Linda.

While Linda slowly sipped the cool drink, Roger brought in reflectors, light enhancing screens, projection screens. "It won't be long," he told Linda and switched on a sensuous Julio Iglesias record. He set up his tripod opposite the sofa and screwed on a very professional looking camera.

"We can project scenes on this fluorescent screen and take your pictures beside palm trees, or a flower bed, or on a movie set. Best to take three or four pictures in day-wear, as you are, another three or four in lingerie in sexy poses and three or four nude art photos."

"I don't know, I don't think so," said Linda hesitantly.

"Listen, ma petite, I understand. You haven't known me for long, it is true. But I am a professional, like a doctor. I discovered in you an exciting new model and I want to bring out the best in you. Girls pay hundreds of dollars to have their pictures taken by professionals. I may be able to sell your pictures to *Penthouse* or *Playboy* and you can get five to ten thousand dollars and have a new career."

Linda kept repeating, "I don't know Roger, I don't think this is for me."

"I have several albums," Roger continued, "but I would never show the pictures to individuals. Only to magazines and only in agreement with the model. These will be your property. There is nothing underhand or shady about this."

Roger just wanted to talk the clothes off Linda. In his experience once he managed to get rid of the clothes, laying the 'model' was not a problem.

Finally Linda said, "Show me a few pictures you've taken. It would help me make up my mind."

Roger repeated that he couldn't do that, because he never showed the pictures to individuals, but when Linda made it a condition of considering posing for Roger, he finally agreed.

"Well, I've never done this before, but some of the girls have left Australia, so it can't hurt them." With this he went to the bedroom. While he was looking for the albums in the wardrobe, he heard a noise. Went to the door and saw Linda leaving the flat. He heard her running down the wooden steps.

Roger ran after Linda and saw her flag down a Radio Cab. He saw the registration number. Went to his own cab and called the base asking them to find out where the cabbie dropped his fare. He told them she left her bag with him and wanted to return it. In about ten minutes he was told that the lady went to the Taxi Club in Flinders Street, Taylor Square.

It was half past eleven when Roger walked up to the first floor hall in the Taxi Club. Dense smoke, whirring of the pokies and loud talk greeted him. The place was crowded with Christmas revellers. He stayed by the entrance and systematically looked over the place to find Linda.

People were moving around, blocking his view but he saw Linda for an instant and immediately moved toward her. Linda noticed him too. She jumped up and hurried toward the toilets. Roger was a couple of metres from her when she disappeared inside.

Roger stood hesitantly in front of the Ladies Room, considering the best mode of action. A woman opened the door, looked at him and went back into the toilet. Roger realised: *Linda will stay inside as long as her 'spies' tell her that I'm still here.* He became angry and pushed in the door. Linda was standing in front of the mirror, clutching her handbag, watching the door.

"Give me back my CDs," said Roger in a strong voice and grabbed the handbag, but Linda tore it away from him.

"Leave me alone," she shouted. "I don't know you. Leave me alone."

By now three ladies were present and they voiced their apprehension forcefully. "Get out of here!" "Leave her alone!" "How dare you break in here!" Roger's explanation fell on deaf ears. "I'll get the manager, he'll throw you out," said one of the women and left.

Roger again tried to move on Linda and grab the handbag, but she hid behind the women who crowded Roger. One of them lifted a heavy handbag and screamed at him. "You lousy bastard, how dare you molest her." They were fighting for their territory and didn't give a damn why Roger came into the Ladies.

The manager and two bouncers entered. He was surprised to see that Roger, whom he knew well, caused the trouble.

"You have to leave immediately," he ordered Roger out.

"Leave him alone," he said to the bouncers who moved in to grab Roger, who kept repeating, "She stole CDs from me. They're in her bag. Check out her bag."

Linda for her part indignantly stated, "I don't know this man, throw him out!"

The manager suspected that Roger would not make a scandal unless he was badly provoked but there was no question that he broke the rules by entering the Ladies toilet.

"Okay, quiet. It's Christmas, for Chrissakes! Leave the Ladies, both of you, right now. If you can settle your problem quietly I'll forget about this. If you make more noise, I'll have you thrown out and I'll take you to the Committee. Out!"

Roger's anger subsided by then but he wanted to get back his CDs. He put his hand on Linda's arm.

"Let's sit down outside and discuss this like adults. I don't care that you conned me and pinched something, but I must have the CDs back. They are part of a collection. You understand?"

She looked at him with weary eyes, keeping her silence, then hesitantly sat down.

"I'll get us some drinks," offered the always gallant Roger. "What'll you have? A screwdriver?" Linda nodded. Roger left, but watched her like a hawk while he waited to be served.

"Okay, show me what you pinched," said Roger, returning with the drinks. Linda just pulled her handbag closer, away from Roger, without saying a word.

"Look, I want to make an offer. I am willing to give you money to get my CDs back. How many did you pinch?" No answer, her lips pressed tight, her eyes became moist.

Roger was always a sucker for female tears. "Well, how many have you got? Two, three, four? Say something, for heaven's sake."

"Three," said Linda quietly. "I wanted to give them to my mother for Chrissie. She loves music." With this her first teardrops fell.

Roger felt like a heel, but there was no way he would let his CDs get away. "Alright, this is my offer. Those CDs cost twenty-nine ninety in the shop. I give you fifteen dollars, half price for each CD, and we forget this whole affair. Here is forty-five dollars. You can buy a present for your mother." He put the money on the table.

Linda hesitated but when she saw that the manager was watching her, she sighed. She took the money first, then pulled out the three CDs and put them on the table. Roger grabbed them and looked at the titles. *Don Carlos, La Traviata and The Marriage of Figaro.* Three of his favourite operas. He felt lucky to get them back.

"Merry Christmas to your mother," he said and left the Club, clutching the CDs.

The Pierce Coulson's
Stories.

Pierce Coulson, Naval Cadet. (Indianapolis)

IT WAS A SUNDAY morning in Indianapolis, USA.

At the end of Sunday Mass in the Chapel of the Naval Institute, Pierce Coulson, Senior Midshipman, started for the gates where he saw people moving about in the bright sunlight in the front of the entrance. Father McAffee was standing just outside the door on the wide landing. He had a good word for everybody.

Pierce's parents were talking to a woman in a light floral dress, a few metres from the door. As she turned, the sun shone through her fine dress and her legs and thighs were clearly outlined under the transparent material.

Pierce stopped and murmured to himself involuntarily, 'What a chassis!' He couldn't make out the face as the bright sunrays blinded him.

"Hello, Pierce," said a familiar, pleasant voice.

"You remember Mrs Chapman, Garry's mother?" said Mrs Coulson seeing the confusion on her son's face.

"Of course he does," said Mrs Chapman. "For a whole year Pierce spent every afternoon at our place trying to hammer algebra into Garry's head. Finally we realised that Garry was not cut out for a career in the Navy. He is now happy, working in a holiday camp. I have to go now. It was so nice to see you all."

Mrs Chapman turned around and the swirl of the light dress around her shapely hips brought back memories that made Pierce blush so deeply that his mother warned him not to stand in the sun any longer.

"I have to go, Mum, Dad, I'll be home for lunch," he said and left.

Pierce headed for the park on the riverbank and sat on the grass in the shade in his white dress uniform.

When was it? Let me see. I was in third form high school. I must have been fifteen. Yes. Garry was in the same form in another class. We were together at athletic training. He was a good all-rounder and a good mate but he had a head like a rock. You couldn't get anything into it, remembered Pierce. Memories came streaming back.

"My parents want me to go to the Naval Academy," said Garry to Pierce one day, "but I can't get this stuff into my head. I am really trying. I stay up all night studying and still can't understand it. Is it true that some of our Presidents flunked mathematics?"

"Yes, they did, but that doesn't mean that you should give it up in third form," said Pierce. "Let me help you. I'll go to your place and show you how to do it. Okay?"

"We can try, but I don't think it will work. Algebra is just all Dutch to me," said Garry.

Gaye Chapman learned from her son that Pierce Coulson would come to her house to help him with his studies. He went every afternoon when they didn't have athletic training. Garry started to make some progress and he was able to get his homework done with Pierce's help. Pierce thought, *with a little luck Garry might be able to pass in Algebra and Mathematics at year's end.*

Mrs Chapman always prepared delicious sandwiches, sweets, and soft drinks for them. She welcomed Pierce when he arrived and fussed about them while they were studying.

"Mum really likes you," said Garry to Pierce. "She never fusses so much when I am studying alone!"

"Your mum is a very nice lady. Nobody can make sandwiches like she can. Not even my mum," said Pierce.

Fifteen-year-old Pierce, who looked eighteen, was having wet dreams about Garry's mother and felt miserable about it. *I shouldn't have dreams like that about my friend's mother. It's not right,* he scolded himself.

Pierce managed to control himself during the day by changing his thoughts when Gaye Chapman's face, or touch came to his mind. But at night it was a different matter.

In his dreams, Gaye Chapman didn't wear an apron and sensible dress like she usually did at home. The dream woman was dancing naked in the meadow, her shapely feet hardly touching the ground. She was coming toward Pierce with inviting open arms and finally descended close to him. She stroked his hair, face, body and gently pulled down his shorts.

When he started to feel the pressure of the shorts on his erect penis, he felt an indescribable mixture of pain and ecstasy and woke up. He felt the sticky fluid flowing on his thighs and onto the bed sheets, making a complete mess of his bed.

"Shit, not again," he cried out in his virgin bedroom and started to wash his bed sheets so that his mother wouldn't notice what had happened.

As he sat in the shade beside the river, the now twenty-year-old Pierce Coulson remembered the first woman in his young life, and felt the uncontrollable hardening again and cried out. "Oh, no! I'm not going to walk around with a wet patch on my white trousers." With this, he sprang to his feet and started to walk fast along the riverbank, absent-mindedly responding to friendly greetings.

No matter how hard he tried, he couldn't get Gaye Chapman out of his mind, especially the afternoon of her fortieth birthday.

He had gone to the Chapman's place to study with Garry. When he knocked, he heard, "It's open, come in. I'm in the living room."

Mrs Chapman was sitting, half-reclining on the sofa in a dressing gown.

"Garry's just left. He had to go to the city to pick up a parcel at the Central Post Office. Come here, sit down," she motioned next to herself.

"I don't want to bother you," said Pierce blushing, desperately trying to block out all his fantasies about the woman who was inviting him to come closer. "You are not bothering me, I wanted to talk to you alone for a long time."

Pierce felt hot, his ears were burning. "Are you all right, Mrs Chapman?" said Pierce looking at her dressing gown which had started to slip off her crossed legs. She was always properly dressed before. *Maybe she is not well* - Pierce thought.

"Oh, I'm all right, just a little tired. Nothing at all. Come on, sit down. What are you afraid of? I'm not going to eat you!"

Pierce wanted to sit down, away from her on the sofa, but she pulled him closer.

"A big man like you, afraid of sitting next to his friend's mother? Shame on you," she said, with a quiet laugh...."Okay, that's better." She held Pierce's hands and turned him to face her.

Pierce felt perspiration all over. His heart was throbbing in his throat and he felt a hard-on. *I'll kill you if you go off now!* He threatened his innocent penis.

"You like Garry a lot, don't you? You wouldn't help him so much if you didn't. Do you like me, too?"

She looked into his eyes, and seeing his wide-eyed admiration and feeling his moist trembling hands, she didn't wait for an answer.

"I am very grateful to you for helping Garry and I like you a lot, too. Do you have a girlfriend?" Pierce shook his head slowly.

"You are still a virgin, aren't you?" Her hands held Pierce tightly now. Pierce pressed his lips together to prevent any sound escaping. He decided he would rather die than answer that question.

"Don't be ashamed, there is a first time for everybody." Her voice was sultry and Pierce could smell her warm breath.

"You made me all excited, you naughty boy. Give me your hand, feel how my heart beats." She pulled Pierce closer and put his hand on her breast. She had nothing on under the dressing gown.

"Look at you, oh my, what have we got there?" She smiled, touching lightly the hard bulge in his trousers and got up from the sofa.

Pierce became a half-conscious dummy and he just let everything happen to him. She guided him to a chair next to the sofa and opened his zipper. She took out his erect penis, and stroked it lightly, then sat on his lap, placing his penis between her thighs. For a couple of seconds she was standing on tiptoe and her body was shaking. She gave a little cry as she pressed herself down on his lap and started to move and grind, moaning.

Pierce never thought a man could feel such pleasure. He had three orgasms by the time she shook violently, pulling his head toward her, kissing his eyes and mouth, while tears ran down her face.

For a short while she sat on his lap, they were still coupled together. She stroked his head, without saying a word. Then she stood up, pulling away with a sigh. In a steady voice she said; "go to the bathroom, wash yourself. Garry will be home soon."

Until this moment, Garry had ceased to exist for Pierce but now the seriousness of what had happened started to gnaw on his conscience. He washed himself quickly. He couldn't face Garry now! Gaye Chapman kissed his face and stroked his hair. "Good bye, Pierce," that was all she said.

For a long while Pierce couldn't look into Garry's eyes, but he didn't notice anything unusual. After that episode Mrs Chapman avoided touching Pierce when he was at their place but otherwise treated him as before. It took two to three months until Pierce finally understood: there were to be no repeats!

Garry passed in Maths and Algebra but dropped the subjects in the following year. The boys met only on the athletic fields afterwards. Pierce had not seen Mrs Chapman in the five years since that exhilarating initiation into manhood until this day.

The Diary of Pierce Coulson Foreign Correspondent. (Sarajevo)

THE SUMMERS OF 1992 and 1993 are burned in my memory for ever.

In 1992, Bruno Fausti, my Italian friend, took me on an Adriatic cruise. We planned to follow the spectacular, mountainous Yugoslav shores southward, down to the Albanian border. The weather was perfect, I lazed in the shade of the mainsail and Bruno sat behind the wheel of his 16 meter yawl, 'Lucifero'. He shouted above the din of the engine. 'This is Ulcinj, the last Yugoslav town. We'll turn back at the Bojana river, the Albanian border.'

I liked what I saw of Ulcinj. Colourful beach umbrellas on the dark volcanic sand gave the place a carnival atmosphere. Sun worshippers, some in the nude, some topless, waved to us as we sailed by.

"Is this a nudist colony?" I asked Bruno.

"No, the nudist colony is in the mouth of the Bojana, on Vada island," Bruno said laughing, winking mischievously.

There was total calm. Only the Lucifero's auxiliary engines broke the peaceful quiet, as we chugged along the shores, passing picturesque small bays enclosed by tall, green trees. Suddenly two shots were fired from the direction of the river mouth. Then more sporadic shots rang out.

"What's going on?" I asked Bruno.

"Probably boar hunting," he said unconcerned.

"We'd better not go any closer. Let's turn back here," I told him, fear nagging at my chest.

A few seconds later Bruno said, "There's somebody in the water." He pointed to a bobbing dark head about two hundred meters away. I picked up my binoculars and found a brown-haired girl swimming erratically, wallowing in the dirty river outlet. Another shot rang out and the bullet missed the girl by some five meters.

My heart raced. "Full throttle ahead, we'll bring her in. Get between her and the shore," I shouted to Bruno.

Without thinking, I dove into the water and swam as fast as I could. When I checked my direction for the second time, I could not see the girl. Bruno shouted something, but I could not make out the words. I pushed myself to swim harder, kept my head in the water and gulped air only when I felt my lungs were about to burst.

I swam another fifty meters, thought I must be almost there and looked up. To my surprise, I saw a small, grey patrol boat about twenty meters away. The World War II vintage boat flew a red flag with the double-headed eagle and the five-pointed star of the Albanians. A soldier stood at water level on a ladder fixed to the side of the boat. He pulled the girl out of the water by her hair.

I treaded water and gulped for air. I heard the girl shout. She struggled to escape from two soldiers who tried to subdue her on the deck of the boat. Her desperate cries spurred me to swim toward the boat as fast as I could.

The soldiers were absorbed with the young woman and paid no attention to me. I looked back and saw the Lucifero approaching.

I climbed up the side of the patrol boat and peered over the edge of the deck. The girl fought and shouted. She was naked. A third soldier held the wheel in the cabin.

I cannot let them take her flashed through my mind. One against three made for bad odds and I realized I would have to surprise them to have any chance at all. I jumped onto the deck, knocked out the soldier on the left with one blow to his chin. I pulled back my arm swiftly and hit the other man with my elbow in the middle of his face, breaking his nose with a satisfying crack. The first soldier slumped over without a sound, the second bent down screaming, smearing blood all over his uniform.

I had no time to lose. I ran to the open cabin where the third soldier turned away from the wheel and reached for his gun. I karate kicked him in the throat and watched him fall into a heap.

The girl lay on the deck. She looked up in bewilderment. Her eyelids opened and closed. I picked her up before she could faint, and jumped into the water. I swam with her to the Lucifero. With Bruno's help we laid her down on the deck. I brought a pair of shorts and a terry cloth gown and dressed her.

She was a young, slender girl, with olive skin. Long, dark hair framed her oval face. Her eyes were closed. I forced her lips open and poured some brandy into her mouth. She coughed and opened her eyes. She looked haunted, like somebody brought back from another world.

The girl said something haltingly, which we did not understand. "You will be all right, you are safe," I told her and Bruno joined in, in Italian. She whispered "thank you," and sighed.

When she regained her composure, she told us her story. Her name was Aida Beganovic. She was sunbathing with friends on the eastern beach of Vada island when a young boy put all her gear in a bucket and, before she could prevent it, he threw the bucket in the river. Aida jumped in to save her things but before she could reach them, Albanian soldiers appeared on the opposite bank and fired shots into the air.

They shouted, "Come out, or we'll shoot you!" She grew frightened and swam toward the sea. There was more shooting. She kept swimming until she felt the water pulling her down. She must have lost consciousness. The pain caused by the soldier yanking her out of the water by her hair brought her around.

Aida was holidaying in Ulcinj, staying in the Hotel Albatros with a German girlfriend called Isolde. She asked to be taken back to Ulcinj.

Bruno knew the Hotel Albatros in Ulcinj well and suggested we should stay the night there. We stayed two days. Aida's exciting natural beauty and the open display of her feelings toward me, made me feel I was in paradise. I wished I could stay longer, but I had already broken the rules. Foreign correspondents were not allowed to enter a country without prior approval of their bosses.

I spent the second night with Aida in her room. Our lovemaking was perfect. I was so aroused by her natural sensuality, I felt I could go on for ever. It was daybreak when nature put an end to the passionate, rhythmic movements of our bodies. I wished I did not have to go and told her I would never forget her. She told me she loved me and asked me to write to her as soon as I could.

"I'll write and I'll see you again. I want to see you again," I answered. I meant every word.

"I work in the Public Relations section in the Sarajevo Town Hall. You can write to me there. We are leaving Ulcinj this morning. This was our last night," she told me.

We embraced and clung together as if we could hold back time as long as we did not let go.

After Aida and Isolde left, Bruno and I finished our journey as we planned and sailed back to Bari. I said good-bye to Bruno and returned to Brussels to report at the NATO Press Section.

I wrote to Aida. I planned to visit her as soon as my assignments would allow. I waited for months, but there was no answer. I had no way of knowing whether she received my letter. Word came to me of heavy-handed censorship in communist Yugoslavia. I wrote to her again and waited for her answer in vain.

In the meantime, we became very busy in Brussels. News of warlike clashes accumulated. First, the declaration of independence by Slovenia prompted threats of military intervention by Belgrade, then Croatia followed suit and the shooting war began. I tried to contact Aida on the phone but the lines of communication were cut. Full scale war erupted and Serbian troops besieged Sarajevo.

When I heard there was a chance to get into Sarajevo with a UN plane delivering medical supplies, I volunteered to go.

In June 1993, we landed at the Sarajevo airport amid the deafening roar of the artillery. Sniper fire peppered our truck as we drove in from the airport. The driver dodged torn down electric wires, building rubble and bomb craters. He dropped me at the building that formerly housed the Olympic Committee and now sheltered a group of foreign correspondents, UN and European Community observers.

Climbing over the debris caused by the unrelenting bombardment, I entered the cellar where a girl distributed press releases to a group of disheveled men and women who represented the world press. She wore jeans and a ski parka. An elastic band at her neck held her long, dark hair. I felt shock and relief as I recognized the girl.

It was Aida.

She did not see me, but must have felt my eyes on her. She turned around and I saw her mouthing my name and she came to me.

"Why did you come? How did you find me?" she asked. Her dark eyes sparkled with joy.

"I cover the war for the Washington Post. Journalists were talking about a girl. They said she's superhuman. It had to be you!"

I looked deep into her beautiful, tired eyes and saw she remembered those two days in Ulcinj. I said, "It's been a whole year. Haven't you received my letters?"

She shook her head and sighed. I touched her hand. That broke the spell.

Reality settled over her. "Do you want some coffee or something to eat?" she asked. She moved to leave but I stopped her.

"The Serbs have gone berserk. With the continuous bombardment and the blockade they'll kill everybody. Those who aren't killed by the shells will die of starvation and disease. I'll take you away!" I could not bear the thought of leaving her behind to face mortal danger.

Her lips turned up slightly, deep sadness showing through her smile. "It's too late," she said. "I'm a Bosnian and would be fighting on the streets with the others, but the Prime Minister ordered me to work with the foreign correspondents. The world must learn the truth. At least we'll break the information blockade."

I tried to convince her that she could do more for Sarajevo in Washington.

"No, this is where I belong. One day the war will be over and we'll have an independent democratic Bosnia," she told me with a brave smile.

While I was desperately searching for a convincing argument to wrench her out of that hellhole, she turned and started for the door.

"I'll get some coffee and bread for you," she said.

I followed her, stepping and jumping over the feet of men and women who had lived in the cellar for days. Aida opened the heavy metal door and the full, horrible cacophony of the battle filled the cellar.

I heard a shout, "Hey you!" Somebody grabbed my arm and held me back while Aida stepped out and closed the door. I pulled myself free and grabbed for the door handle. At that moment, a terrible explosion shook the building and knocked me to the ground. Everything went black.

When I came to, my eyes were caked with dirt. My ears rang. Dust-covered figures moved silently around me in a ghostly pantomime. I tried to pry the door open but could not. A Yugoslav Air Force bomb had hit the building directly. Only those sheltered in the cellar survived.

The thunder of nearby collapsing buildings caused the ground to tremble under my feet. It was not just bricks and stones that lay in rubble around me that horrifying day.

I thought I heard the clatter of hooves, as the horsemen of the Apocalypse rode away carrying with them Aida's young life, and our future, leaving me with only memories and a deep ache.

Pierce Coulson US Intelligence Officer. (London)

THE DOWNSTAIRS DINING ROOM of the Indian restaurant in Oxford Street, central London was opulent. To Dorothea, the sensuous vermillion and gold patterns conjured up pictures of the days of the British Raj from the stories her relatives told her.

"I'll leave ordering to you, you know the place," said Pierce, the American Liaison Officer she'd met the day before at an official function. Dorothea studied the menu and Pierce studied her.

The blending of round arches, curved furniture, flowing colour patterns, the subdued, monotonous chatter of the diners and silent movements of the staff effected a kind of magic.

Pierce felt he was alone with Dorothea on a raft, carried on the waves of emotions toward a widening horizon. *Who is this beautiful, intelligent, very proper English woman, radiating sensuality while sitting here in her tweed outfit, her thick, dark hair pulled up in a bun? Has she got some aristocratic English public servant, or lawyer lover, screwing her once a month on a certain day that fits their timetable?*

Dorothea was looking at the menu, but she was also reading her own mind. She felt something new. With her first lover, Peter Farrell, a fellow student at Oxford University, she was committed without hesitation but Pierce attracted and frightened her at the same time.

Why am I comparing Pierce to Peter? Is Peter a yardstick to measure other men by? He betrayed me; he used me as a plaything while it suited him. Anybody should come out looking good compared to Peter, she thought bitterly.

But Dorothea was deluding herself. She had loved Peter, and she yearned for the feeling of being in love again.

She was watching herself as she analyzed her feelings toward Pierce. She did like Pierce at first sight when they met at the British-American Intelligence Liaison meeting, but as soon as she became aware of that, she withdrew into her shell to avoid getting hurt.

Is this what I am going to do for the rest of my life? Keep away from men I like and become 'one of the boys' at the office? Is it better to have loved and lost than never to have loved at all? she asked herself. She wondered if she agreed with Tennyson, or she was using his lines as a stick to lean on, while she waited for her heart to make the decision.

"Are you ready to order?" asked the waiter, but Dorothea didn't hear him.

Pierce understood that she was considering other things, not the menu. He cleared his throat.

"I'd like beef vindaloo, medium hot with condiments. What do you fancy, Dorothea?" he asked gently, not to startle her.

The spicy food forced them to eat slowly; and to soothe its sting they drank the excellent Pont Neuf Noir which Pierce had ordered.

Pierce had surprised Dorothea at the end of the official Intelligence Liaison meeting when he produced two theatre tickets and Dorothea surprised herself when she agreed to stay in London to see *Educating Rita* and have supper with him after the show. The Indian restaurant was Dorothea's idea. Later she wondered about her choice.

Did I think the special occasion called for a special treat?

"The play was a variation on the Pygmalion theme, wasn't it?" said Pierce.

"You could say that," agreed Dorothea. "The professor, out of the goodness of his heart and sheer curiosity, took on the education of the simple girl only to find out that she knew more about life than he did."

"It seemed a fairly typical English play to me," ventured Pierce.

"You mean outdated attitudes served up in a rehashed version?" said Dorothea and sipped her wine.

"Please, don't be offended. That's not what I meant. I really admire the British preference for fair play as opposed to the win-at-all-costs attitude, which could be called the American way."

Maybe he isn't the prototype American I thought he was. At least I should give him a fair hearing before I sentence him, mused Dorothea.

"Why did you go to work at the Government Communications Headquarters? I could picture you better in foreign service representing your country," said Pierce.

"I was going to work for the Foreign Office, that's why I graduated in Slavic languages and European history."

"Why did you change your mind? They made you an offer you couldn't refuse?"

"Hardly. My father directed me to go "where Britannia could make the best use of me". He was in Naval Intelligence and the services were short of British-born East-European experts, who spoke the languages too."

"Now I know why I felt so close to you from the beginning." He filled her glass.

"Cheers, to our common roots. My family is Navy through and through too."

"To the eternal ties of all sailors and their descendants," he clinked his glass to Dorothea's.

"How did you get into Naval Intelligence?" she asked.

"Straight as an arrow. Indianapolis, a tour of duty on the South China Sea, Master Degree in Electronic Communication, the works."

"Well, our roots are similar and probably our motivations too. A sense of duty and vigilance."

The wine, the excitement of being on a date with the handsome American untied Dorothea's tongue.

"Where did you get that cut above your right eye, Pierce?" she asked suddenly.

Pierce knew that the question was a sign of her interest in him.

"Would you believe," he asked with a quixotic smile, "that I was dropped from a chopper on a P.T. boat floundering on the South China Sea after they lost the captain and the first mate, I saved the men and the boat and got only this scratch in the process."

"I'd believe it if you were serious, but it looks more like a sporting accident. Basketball, or boxing?" she asked playfully.

"Yes, I did some boxing at the Academy."

Pierce drank a full glass of wine to wash away the memories of the night on the South China Sea, where he did exactly what he'd just told her.

Before they knew it, it was midnight and the restaurant prepared to close. Pierce walked Dorothea to the Duchess Mews apartment kept by her office for occasions when they had to stay in London overnight.

They chatted like old friends during the short walk. As they approached her place, Dorothea's thoughts concentrated on the question: *How should this perfect evening end? How will we part, what should I say and more importantly, do, to give him the right signals?*

She liked him, enjoyed the evening and wanted to see him again. But she would not jump into bed with this handsome, sexy man just because her hormones urged her. It had been such a long time since her last relationship, she had almost forgotten how to give the right signals to a man. She was startled to realize they were standing at the gate.

Pierce read her mind and thought her precious enough to wait for. He didn't want to spoil his chances with Dorothea for the few months he would be in England.

"Thank you for the lovely evening," she said.

"We should do it more often," said Pierce and looked into her eyes, searching for the answer to the only question he was interested in. *Does she want me as much as I want her?*

Oh, God, he will ask me to let him in for a night-cap, and I couldn't do that here, even if I wanted to. The janitor would report me. The thoughts raced through Dorothea's mind. She felt dizzy and started to fumble in her handbag, though she didn't have the keys to the gates.

Pierce stepped closer and gently lifted her face. He saw the answer in her eyes. Yes, she wanted him too, but she was not ready to act yet. Pierce kissed her. First gently, then passionately. She kissed him back, in a dreamlike state.

A light came on and the janitor approached, clanging large, old keys. "Sweet dreams, Your Highness," said Pierce alluding to the name of the place. Dorothea just waved and disappeared behind the wrought iron gate.

She is a lady, but she will give herself to you, buddy, because she wants you, Pierce consoled himself with. He whistled on his way to his Bryanston Square flat.

For a month or so Coulson's amorous plans with Dorothea seemed to falter. He rang her on three or four occasions and got the same answer. "I'd like to see you too, but for some time I will not have a moment to myself. It's work related."

Tibor Vajda

Is she really that busy, or have I frightened her off, Pierce wondered, thinking over the details of their last meeting.

A month had passed when Dorothea decided to meet with Pierce in London again and reminded herself to take a change of clothing and her sexy nightie. She was sure of staying the night in London, but she chased away her thoughts when the question came up of whether she would make love to Pierce this time. *I don't want to plan it,* she told herself.

Before contacting him, she received a fax from Pierce. It was addressed to her and it said: "Dear Ms Cruikshank, see what you can make of this and please advise me what do you think of its content."

For an hour or so she tried the usual methods to decode the message but she got nowhere with it.

Finally she decided to bite the bullet and asked a woman friend in Division H (Decoding) of the Government Communications Head Quarters at Cheltenham, to put the message through the number-cruncher for her 'in tea-time', without officially recording the content.

Dorothea received the decoded message the next day.

"The code: Simple number/letter substitution. Text:

Mayday, Mayday, Mayday

Let me love you, please.

Yours, Pierce."

He tricked me with this 'boy-scout' code she told herself with a smile and looked around to see if her co-workers were watching.

She then phoned her London secretary to call Commander Coulson at the American Embassy and ask him to come to her London Office. She was ready for Pierce.

96

Rape Of The Inca Empire.
(Spain - Peru)

IN 1493, IN ORDER to head off a war between Spain and Portugal over discoveries in the New World, Pope Alexander VI divided the territory with an imaginary 'line of demarcation'.

Almost 40 years after this papal decree, soldier of fortune Francisco Pizarro set out for Peru to secure the pagan kingdom of the Incas for Charles V, King of Spain, and the Catholic Church.

‡‡

"Look at those two Franciscos," said Maribella Orellana to Francisca Pizarro standing next to her in front of the gate to her yard in Trujillo of the Estremadura in Spain.

"Like brothers, though not twins," she said and sighed as she pointed at the two boys, Francisco Pizarro and Francisco Orellana. They were driving the small herd of pigs out to the meadow of the Sierra de Gata looming directly behind Trujillo.

"They might be half-brothers, if your Francisco was fathered by the same Hidalgo who fathered my four bastardos but you never let anybody know who knocked you up, like it was a big shame or something," burst out Francisca Pizarro.

"God sent me Francisco. I don't share him with anybody, certainly not with these vagabonds. He is all mine," said Maribella Orellana and with that the conversation was over.

The women turned their backs to the road and with a small wave of their hands stepped back into their neighbouring yards, closing the gates behind them.

Francisco Pizarro was born in Trujillo, Spain in 1476. His life started out in poverty. Like most of the country-people at the time, he never learned to read and write. He tended to his father's pigs. His father was Gonzalo Pizarro Rodriguez de Aguilar, an Infantry Captain, a poor Hidalgo, an impoverished noble of the lower class, who never married the mother of his children.

Francisco Pizarro joined the Spanish military as soon as he was able to and fought in the Hispaniola Island War against the Italians. When the war ended he volunteered to sail with Alonso de Ojeda, one of the first conquistadors to set out for the Indies.

Pizarro's alliance with Ojeda took him to Jamaica where he heard tales of great wealth to be found in El Dorado, somewhere along the western coast of South America.

Pizarro decided to form his own company of explorers with the help of Diego de Almagro, another conquistador with whom he would have a long and precarious partnership. The two men obtained funding from Spanish Emperor Charles V with the promise that they would keep little gold for themselves and send most of it back to Spain.

When Pizarro landed in Peru in 1532, all he knew of the Incas was that, according to legend, they possessed fabulous wealth. His twin objectives were to loot the empire and to subjugate its people to Christianity and Spanish rule.

However, in many ways Inca civilization was more advanced than Western Europe's at the time. Inca physicians were performing successful brain surgeries while their European counterparts still prescribed leeches for just about every ailment.

Inca architecture, agriculture and astronomy had progressed remarkably too, but perhaps the most amazing Inca achievements concerned social order. In their society there were no poor people. Widows, orphans, and invalids were cared for by the state. Workers retired at age 50 on pensions of food and clothing. There was little crime because every basic need was met. At the head of this benevolent system was the ruler, the Inca, who demanded in exchange the obedience of his subjects.

The conquistadors had arrived at a most opportune time for their purpose. Both Atahualpa and his half-brother Huascar had claimed the throne after their father, Huayna Capac, died in 1525 without formally naming his successor. Although Capac's priest designated Huascar the ruler, a civil war erupted between the two brothers and lasted until 1532 when Atahualpa's forces captured and imprisoned Huascar.

Huascar was forced to witness the slaughter of the royal family. Hundreds of women, men and children were killed so Atahualpa could reign without the danger of further challenge.

Atahualpa's bloody power play disrupted the well-ordered Inca society and the natives hailed Pizarro when he arrived, believing that he was the son of their white-skinned God Viracocha who was sent to avenge Huascar and his family. The sound of his cannon added credence to Pizarro's false identity, since Viracocha 'controlled the thunder', according to Inca legend. As the conquistadors plundered their way across the country, they met with no resistance from the thoroughly intimidated and demoralized Incas.

However, when word of the Spaniards' conduct during their trek to Cajamarca reached Atahualpa he demanded that the 'thieves' return the goods they had stolen. Instead, Pizarro sent him a priest, Brother Vicente, who proceeded to lecture Atahualpa in the Catholic religion.

The catechism lesson ended abruptly when Atahualpa hurled the Bible on the ground saying that 'it did not speak to him'. At this, the offended Spaniards – who had been whipped into a religious frenzy by Pizarro the previous night – attacked and slaughtered the unarmed natives.

The Inca warriors were stationed outside the city, scattered by the onslaught of the Spanish artillery. Atahualpa was taken captive and held for ransom. When he learned that Huascar was promising the Spanish more gold than he did for his own release, the ruthless Atahualpa secretly ordered his brother's death.

During the next nine months, gold and silver to fill two rooms was delivered to Pizarro to secure Atahualpa's safe return to the throne, but the Spaniard broke his promise to Atahualpa. He had no intention of releasing his prisoner. Pizarro knew that in order to disrupt and conquer this well-run society, he must kill the Inca leader.

After a mock trial, at which Pizarro and Almagro were the judges, Atahualpa was found guilty of the charge that he ordered to kill his own brother and fomented revolt against the Spaniards. Pizarro offered him a choice: he could elect to be 'burned alive as a heathen' or to be 'strangled as a Christian'.

The Inca ruler chose the latter. He was baptized Juan de Atahualpa in honour of St. John the Baptist. Then he was tied to a stake and garrotted. Pizarro and his men gave the Inca a full-scale Catholic funeral.

Even with the Incas virtually decimated, Pizarro was still beset with problems. While he expanded his conquest, other conquistadors challenged his territory.

Pizarro once again enlisted the help of Almagro. Almagro was reluctant to help because despite his original deal with Pizarro that they divide the spoils of the Incas equally he had yet to see any profit.

Pizarro convinced him that he could have all of Chile if he would help. Almagro agreed only to find that he was cheated again. In retaliation he seized the city of Cuzco.

A year later, Pizarro invaded Cuzco with indigenous troops and with it sealed the conquest of Peru. The conquest was a gruesome one filled with bloodshed, plunder and savagery. Several Spanish men had raped Indian women, including Pizarro who violated the wife of Manco Inca, the new ruler, or Inca.

Pizarro then founded the city of Lima in Peru's central coast on January 18, 1535, a foundation that he considered one of the most important things he had created in his life.

After the final effort of the Inca to recover Cuzco had been defeated by Almagro, a dispute occurred between him and Pizarro respecting the limits of their jurisdiction. This led to confrontations between the Pizarro brothers and Almagro, who was eventually defeated during the Battle of Las Salinas (1538) and executed.

In Lima on June 26, 1541, a group of twenty heavily armed supporters of the younger Almagro stormed Pizarro's palace, assassinated him, and then forced the terrified city council to appoint young Almagro as the new Governor of Peru. He was then caught and executed the following year.

‡‡

Francisco de Orellana, Pizarro's friend (and possibly his half-brother) was born in Trujillo like Pizarro himself.

Orellana was sixteen years old when he travelled to both Panama and Nicaragua. In 1553 he continued on to explore Peru with Francisco Pizarro.

Orellana's motto was 'Never give up!' as he confirmed it in his poetic autobiography:

He loved discovery, explorations and adventure
He felt courageous, inquisitive, ambitious and clever
He believed anything was possible
He explored the full course of the Amazon river
He gained happiness, notoriety and power
Resident of Spain
Who always said 'Never give up'.

Orellana led two journeys to the Amazon. His first journey explored the full course of the Amazon river. It actually happened as an accident when Pizarro, with whom Orellana was travelling asked Orellana to travel down the river to get provisions so that Pizarro and his crew could continue with their expedition.

Orellana initially sailed down the Napo river which is a tributary of the Amazon. After landing, Orellana found it difficult to get back upstream to deliver the provisions. He was unable to return to Pizarro so he continued downstream.

While going downstream, Orellana encountered many Indian tribes. He found much valuable cinnamon and gold. He also encountered some 'oversized women' who reminded him of the Amazons of Greek legends who were a warrior tribe of women.

After he was attacked by these Amazon warrior women, he named the river the Amazon river.

On his journey he had only 50 Spaniards and one small brigantine ship to travel the river for one year. They practically had to rebuild their small ship to be able to return with it to Spain.

On Orellana's second trip he managed to convince the Spanish government to finance the journey. They gave him 400 men and four ships to exploit the riches of the 'Amazon people' but the second journey was not a success. After many Indian attacks Orellana lost one eye. He succumbed to tropical diseases and died in 1546. Only some crew members and his wife Maria made it back safely to Spain.

‡‡

It was an early Thursday morning in the autumn of 2007 in Trujillo, the Spanish town of Estremadura. The two tired elderly travellers Fernando de Orellana Pizarro and Juan Pizarro de Orellana woke up, gingerly trying to move their weary bones. Sleeping the night on a granite slab bench in the shadow of the equestrian statue of the Conquistador Francisco Pizarro made them stiff and sore.

The first rays of the sun struggled to break through the cloud cover as they shone on the people who moved through the Plaza Mayor to set up their market stalls outside the city walls. The five-hundred-year old tradition of the Thursday morning markets was reborn.

"Look at the place. Our forefathers left a village and we returned to a town. Our great-great-great-grandfather can be proud looking down at his own statue. This is Spain, you can see the difference between the Peruvian mestizos, who chased us out calling the glorious conquistadores thieves and murderers and the Spaniards who are proud of being from the race of the conquerors and their discoveries of the New World. Look at all these palaces and castles, with the escudos (shields) of the families above the doors.

"There is one thing that has never changed. Look at the stork-nests on the roof of the old church, next to the clock-tower. We heard so many stories about them in the family. The dandy storks will soon begin their winter return to warmer African climates just to come back in the spring. Remember the tales about the storks?"

"I remember, I remember, the place is fine, but to feel finally home again we'll have to find a place where we can put our heads down. We have to find the old Pizarro house and our distant relatives. I trust the blood of the Pizarros and of the Orellanas hasn't turned to water and they'll be happy to see us. Don't you think so?"

"Of course I do. I wouldn't have come this far if I didn't! Let's ask the locals where can we find our ancestral homes. They used to be on the top of the hill. They didn't move the house, I'm sure of that, but these new zig-zagging streets are hiding the road leading to them."

The two men followed the direction pointed out to them by a man hurrying to the market. After leaving the Plaza Mayor, about half-way up the hill, they found the magnificent palace fortress, the Palacio de Juan Orellana. There was no sign of life around the place. "Those who don't go to the market don't get up so early," explained Juan. As Juan wanted to knock on the gate Fernando stopped him.

"I can see 'our house' a little further up on the hill. People are moving about. Let's check that out first," he said and moved on, dragging Juan with him.

The rebuilt house of the Pizarros, another palace fortress, had comfortable living quarters on the ground floor and a small museum upstairs.

Donna Maria Francesca received the weary travellers as true blood-relative would, and allocated them one room of the 'museum'. She was particularly proud when they told her that it was through another Francesca, great-granddaughter of the Conquistador Francisco Pizarro that the Pizarro and the Orellana families tied their relationship.

The day passed fast. Everybody in the neighbourhood wanted to see the famous travellers, shake their hands and listen to their stories about the adventures they had during their voyage back to Spain from the other side of the world. They brought them food and kept milling around until Donna Francesca ordered the travellers to retire to their room.

Sleep and dreams came fast. Memories of their past, the legends and stories they heard, were woven into a colourful tapestry that appeared to them as the true picture of their own life.

‡‡

In a belated confession Pope Benedict XVI said in Brazil, on the 11th of May, 2007 (L.A. Times): "It is impossible to ignore the unjustified crimes that accompanied evangelisation here, in the 15th and 16th centuries."

About the Author:

- -

TIBOR TIMOTHY VAJDA WAS born in Budapest, Hungary. He emigrated with his family to Australia in 1956, and settled in Sydney. Vajda was registered and practiced as a Surgeon Dentist from 1962-1993. After an internationally successful clinical and academic career in Oral Implantology and Biomedical Engineering he turned to full-time writing.

In his writing Vajda uses the information he absorbed in his Psychology, History, Geography and Politics studies in five languages during his frequent round the world trips.

By 2011 Vajda published eleven books and more than two dozens short stories in Australia and the United States and in the UK. He has received several Awards in Short Story Competitions.